T0072522

EVERYTHING UNDER THE CLOUDS

Janoesha Harbour Book 4

M C Williams

BALBOA.PRESS

A DIVISION OF HAY HOUSE

Balboa Press books may be ordered through booksellers or by contacting:

Balboa Press
A Division of Hay House
1663 Liberty Drive
Bloomington, IN 47403
www.balboapress.com
844-682-1282

Because of the dynamic nature of the Internet, any web addresses or
links contained in this book may have changed since publication and
may no longer be valid. The views expressed in this work are solely those
of the author and do not necessarily reflect the views of the publisher,
and the publisher hereby disclaims any responsibility for them.

The author of this book does not dispense medical advice or prescribe the use
of any technique as a form of treatment for physical, emotional, or medical
problems without the advice of a physician, either directly or indirectly. The
intent of the author is only to offer information of a general nature to help
you in your quest for emotional and spiritual well-being. In the event you use
any of the information in this book for yourself, which is your constitutional
right, the author and the publisher assume no responsibility for your actions.

Any people depicted in stock imagery provided by Getty Images are
models, and such images are being used for illustrative purposes only.
Certain stock imagery © Getty Images.

Print information available on the last page.

ISBN: 978-1-9822-7401-6 (sc)
ISBN: 978-1-9822-7402-3 (e)

Balboa Press rev. date: 09/07/2021

CONTENTS

MAIN CHARACTERS

1. Hayden Alexander
2. James Morris
3. Dee-dee Simmons
4. Byron Phelps
5. Ravi Esnor
6. Matt Davis
7. Lorne Mater
8. Kimberly Anrhime
9. Madam Zebandee
10. Ann Miller
11. Christine Namandi
12. Jacob Pilzner
13. Ben Hammerlay
14. Stella Xavier
15. Stacey Lane
16. Moses Uatobuu
17. Ronald Gosslett
18. Terry Willis
19. Dana Hollinger
20. Morris Elgin
21. Lisa Namamak
22. Joe Shilo
23. John Moawabae
24. Rose Teltin
25. Oscar Rambuutae
26. Leann Greggs
27. Dean Ogammi
28. Jeff Embree
29. Prussian Aubern
30. Al Foster

1

October 2ⁿᵈ, 2021 Brookshore, Janoesha Harbour

The last flick just finished for the night at the BTM
on the PBP and it's costumers were empting out into
the streets, some heading home and some heading
down to Tilliquimsara to watch the bonfire and listen
to music. Fifty-two year old Dee-dee Simmons came
to the movies with a friend of her's from work, it
was classic night at the Big Ticket Movie theater
along the beach, they chose the movie Purple Noon,
Dee-dee remembers as a little girl having a crush on
Alain Delon, she thought he had the most beautiful
eyes and smile, she giggled at the memory of that.
She had just said bye to her girlfriend Beth, they had
parted ways on the front steps of the theater, Dee-dee
headed south on the PBP to a variety store to get a

pack of cigarettes. She bought her smokes and came out of the store and started walking up Mellongrove Avenue, it was her short-cut to get to the InnerHoop station. Mellongrove is a small street that branches off the PBP and heads west, its a quiet neighborhood of bungalows which in the night can seem a little dark and drarry. Dee-dee opened her pack of cigarettes as she walked up the street, she took one out of the pack and lit it, inhaling the smoke into her lungs and out her nose, she took a few more puffs as she kept walking. She heard shuffling of feet nearby then bushes crackling, Dee-dee looked around but saw nothing she grew concerned and quickened her pace just then a hand went over her mouth and someone dragged her into a small patch of bushes in a open lot and started stabbing her as she screamed out in terror begging for her life.

The next day opened up with blue skies and lots of sunshine, the JBI office in Brookshore was starting a new day a lot of its employees was at the nearby coffee shop getting perked up for the day. Fofty-eight year old Hayden Alexander is a Profiler that works out of the Behavioral Science Division of the JBI, he's currently stuck in traffic on the PBP.

Hayden is quite wealthy, his dad was a Rig Mechanic from Cairo, Egypt that started up his own business when he came to Janoesha Harbour and now owns a franchise of garages from here to

Egypt. His mother was a Grade 12 Math Teacher from Plymouth, Tobago, his parents met on Janoesha Harbour in 1968. Hayden went to the University Of Janoesha Harbour in Alan's Landing he majored in Behavioral Science & Criminology.

He did his best to get up early and try to beat the morning rush but no such luck, everyone was thinking like he was, now he was stuck in traffic in his 1952 emerald-green Rolls Royce Silver Wraith limousine. "Sorry sir there's no way I can get out of this" Ravi his chauffeur said "don't worry it's not your fault" Hayden replied, just then an announcement came over the police-radio he had installed in the limo it said that there was a body found in a vacant lot on Mellongrove Avenue. "Sir we're not too far from that location do you want me to take a detour" Ravi asked "if you can" Hayden replied, Ravi maneuvered the limo into a small space to his left provided for him from the gods, after getting into that small space he was able to exit off the freeway and onto Coral Road that ran parallel with the PBP. He headed back south to get onto Mellongrove Avenue, it didn't take him that long to find the street, the GPS indicated to make a left on Mellongrove Avenue so Ravi complied. As they turned onto Mellongrove Avenue they could see police cars and a Coroner's van he also noticed that the rest of his unit was already there. There were officers putting up police tape so that nosy and concerned neighbors didn't get too close, Ravi parked at a reasonable distance away. Hayden opened the door and stepped out of the car, as he stood up straight on the sidewalk he straightened up his smokey-gray denim sports jacket and took his JBI badge out of the front pocket of his black pleated dress pant and hooked it on his belt. Hayden walked up to the chief of police for Brookshore and showed him his badge "Hayden Alexander Profiler for the JBI's Behavioral Science Division" he said to the chief and extended his hand as a greeting "Major Byron Phelps nice to meet you" Byron shook his hand. "What happened here" Hayden asked him, Byron walked Hayden over to where the body was, the coroner had covered it with a blanket "some kids playing in the neighborhood stumbled upon the body" Byron told him. Hayden stooped down next to the body "how long since the murder" Hayden asked "the coroner said nine to ten hours" Byron replied as he gave Hayden a strange look "how do you know she was murdered" he asked Hayden "she's missing her tongue and she has a ligature mark around her neck plus I count at lease twenty stab wounds to her breast and stomach" Hayden replied. "One of your partners is coming right now" Byron informed Hayden, Hayden looked up to see Profiler James Morris standing over top of him "hey Jim how you doing" Hayden asked "could be better" James replied. "Looks like the same doer as the body up in Umni" James said "if so this is the fourth one in three weeks" Hayden replied "the chief said they found her shorts in some bushes but her panties are still missing" James informed Hayden. Hayden spotted a pack of cigarettes in the corpse's right hand "that looks like a new pack" Hayden said to James as he pointed at the pack of smokes, James checked the pack "only one missing" James informed Hayden 'maybe someone saw her just before she got killed' Hayden thought to himself "isn't there a variety store at the end of this street on the PBP" Hayden asked James "yeah Shore & Breeze Variety it's open 24 hours" James replied "maybe someone there saw her or her killer they could also have surveillance cameras" Hayden informed James. James got two uniformed officers to go to the variety store and find out if they have video or camera surveillance and to wait there until they got there. Byron came back over to where Hayden and James was "the coroner said to give this to you" Byron said to Hayden as he gave him the dead woman's wallet. Hayden checked her ID it said that her present address is in Amaryllis Jaiz, she also had work ID from a Slaps Bed and Breakfast where she worked as a cook "Dee-dee Gail Simmons born August 17th, 1969" Hayden read as he looked at a picture ID of her "someone's missing a wife or a mother" James added. The coroner finally moved the body from the open lot and brought it to the JBI lab where they can do testing for any foreign DNA or unknown skin under her fingernails. "I'll stay here and check out the variety store you head to the lab, maybe the killer left his DNA on her" Hayden told James, James went in the back of the coroner's van and left with them. Hayden also knew that he had to take a road trip to Amaryllis Jaiz "can you get some men to bag some of this dirt up" Hayden asked Byron as he looked around the crime scene for evidence "sure thing" Byron replied "chief" Hayden called over to Byron before he could gather up some men "yeah" Byron said as he turned around to face him "did you find any weapons" Hayden asked "no nothing to my knowledge" Byron replied. Hayden stood up straight from being crouched down he took off the rubber gloves that he had put on ten minutes earlier and stuffed them in his jacket pocket, he headed back up to where his limo was "hey are you leaving" Byron called to him "I'm heading to the variety store" Hayden told him "what do I do with the dirt" Byron asked "send it to our crime lab" Hayden replied as he made his way to his limo. At the limo Ravi was in the driver's seat listening to classical music, a piano concharto from Sleun on blue-ray, Ravi was in keystroke bliss with the tranquility of the Baby-grand and its pleasant sounds, Hayden cot him imitating a band leader waving his hands around to the sound of the music and humming to himself with his eyes closes until he opened his eyes and saw Hayden staring at him through the car's window, that made him jump in his seat.

James went with the coroner back to the lab, when they got to the lab they transported the body on a gurney from the van to one of the labs in the basement of the JBI building. James texted Hayden to let him know that he was at the lab, James put on a lab-mask over his mouth and nose, the coroner and his helper rolled the body off the gurney and onto a steel table that had a drain built in one of its corners. As they did that James spotted something that he didn't notice at the crime scene "hold on do you see that" he said to the coroner as he pointed at her neck "her head is almost decapitated" he told the coroner "how did we miss that" he asked the coroner "it's so fine a cut that we didn't see it" the coroner told James as he studied the corpse's neck "it also looks like she might have been strangled" his helper added "why do you say that" James asked him "because if you look you can see bruising on both sides of the lower jaw which look like knuckle impressions" he explained to James. The coroner was collecting any foreign material or biological fluid from the body before he washed it down, "it looks like she was raped" the coroner said "where do you see that" James asked him "look here" the coroner showed James as he had him come in for a closer look "see how there's stripping in the vaginal area" the coroner told him. James saw something that didn't seem right "what are those black specks" James asked the coroner as he pointed to the vaginal area "I'm not too sure, I'll collect some for testing" the coroner replied.

Ravi backed the Rolls Royce into a parking spot in front of the Shore & Breeze Variety Store, the store had a couple self-serve gas pumps out front a small diner was attached to the right section of the store. "I'll be right back" Hayden told Ravi as Ravi put the car in park "is there anything you want while I'm in there" Hayden asked him "maybe something to drink" Ravi replied.

Ravi was born Ravi Ernest Esnor on July 22nd, 1985, his mom was a store clerk from Goa, India and his dad was a paralegal from Canterbury, England. His parents met on Janoesha Harbour in 1976 and are now at the present time retired and living in Tamerra. Ravi followed in his father's footsteps and studied paralegal at Hamner College in Alan's Landing he graduated with honors and later worked as a paralegal for eight years at Rogel & Burns law firm. He quit after the owners got cot for embezzlement and found a job as a chauffeur driving around a JBI Profiler.

Hayden left the limo and headed into the variety store, a few bells chimed as he pushed the front door to the store open, there was no one in the store just the clerk a customer playing a stack of scratch and win tickets and the two uniformed police officers. Hayden looked around as he stepped in the store, he saw where the clerk was and went over to the counter he was standing behind, the two officers left the store and stood post outside as Hayden moved closer to the counter "hi sir how are you today" Hayden said to the clerk "not bad but it's not sir it's Al Foster nice to meet you" Al replied as he extended his hand in friendship, Hayden shook his hand. "Sorry Al my name is Hayden Alexander I'm a Profiler for the JBI we're investigating a crime that happened nearby here" Hayden said as he showed Al his ID and badge "if I can help I sure will" Al told him. Hayden showed him the picture ID of Dee-dee "have you seen this lady" he asked Al, Al took a look at the picture "yeah I have" he said and continued "she came in last night around midnight and bought a lighter and a pack of smokes" Al replied "are you sure it was her" Hayden inquired "yeah it was her I remember because she didn't have enough change until this guy gave her some" Al told him "was she with anyone" Hayden asked "no she was alone" Al replied "the guy that gave her the change what did he look like" Hayden inquired "sorry I didn't get a good look at him he was wearing a hoodie, all I know he was tall and white" Al said "how long after she left did that guy leave" Hayden asked "not too long after maybe five minutes or less" Al replied "did you happen to see what vehicle he was driving" Hayden asked "no sorry I didn't but I was going to call the police earlier that night about a black Mustang that was parked across the street for three hours nobody got out of the car and the windows were tinted so dark you couldn't see in it, it just seemed creepy to me" Al said "did you see that car later on that night" Hayden inquired "no after that I never saw it again" Al replied "does your surveillance-cameras work" Hayden asked as he pointed at one of the two surveillance-cameras he had mounted on the wall behind the counter "no they're just for show" Al replied. Hayden put away Dee-dee's ID and handed Al one of his business cards "thanks for your time Al if you think of anything that can help us please don't hesitate to call" he told Al, Hayden grabbed a soda pop from the fridge and paid for it before he left. When he got back to his car he knocked on the driver's side window the window went down "here's your drink" Hayden said as he handed Ravi the soda "thank you sir" Ravi replied and put the soda in the limo's glove compartment. Hayden got into the backseat and shut the door "where to now sir" Ravi asked "lets head to the office" Hayden replied.

In an open field just southwest of Mollymawk Marina stood a old brick house that had a chain-linked fence around its property, from the main road it was hard to see the house it was partially hidden behind an abandon factory. Inside the house lived fifty-two year old Terry Willis, he was a Taxidermist who was relieved of his position from the Passco Regional Museum in Brookshore he now works on his own from his home. Inside his house has various animal heads mounted on the walls, in the living room the shelves were filled with books about hunting and the human anatomy, the cupboards in the kitchen had in them pickle jars with human tongues in them soaking in formaldehyde. Behind a desk in the living room is where he did his work, only a handful of clients came by who gave him repeated business, Terry usually kept to himself his social life was spent at the local bar playing trivia on the small computers that were stored behind the bar, he would sit at the end of the bar away from any crowd of people and sip on a glass of scotch on the rocks.

Hayden met up with James at the JBI building in Brookshore, a team of profilers which was headed by Hayden was in a board room going over the Dee-dee Simmons murder case. They were coming up with a profile of the Unsub, the name Unsub is short for unknown subject, Hayden's profiling team consisted of Technical Analysis Lorne Mater, Communications Liaison Kimberly Anrhime, Junior Profiler Matt Davis and Senior Profiler James Morris. "This body has the same calling-card as the one in Umni she was missing her tongue" Hayden informed his team "I found a ticket stub in her blouse pocket for the Big Ticket

Movie theater for the late showing of Purple Noon, maybe someone at the theater knows something" James said "okay this is good, Matt and James you check out the theater, Kimberly start drafting up a profile of the unsub that we can bring to the police station and Lorne check to see if there has been any cases with this signature in the past, I'm heading to Amaryllis Jaiz to speak with the owner of Slaps Bed & Breakfast" Hayden told his team. Kimberly wasn't too sure where to start with the profile "where do I start" she asked Hayden "The unsub we're looking for is cold and calculating with a macob sense of humor a true sociopath void of any feelings and I can almost guarantee you that he will strike again, he is no fool and he is a person that studies his prey, he's patient and he has perfected his art" Hayden told her. "We know he kills cross city lines what if he does it across regional lines to" Matt inquired "Lorne's working on that right now" Hayden said "the only news outlet that is airing the case is our local channel twelve I'm working at keeping it that way for now" Kimberly informed Hayden, "thank you Kim" Hayden said to her. "Okay everybody you all know what to do it's going to be a long day so get some caffeine in you" Hayden told his team as he got up from around the table, he headed to the elevator with James and Matt following behind him. Hayden was intercepted before he went in the elevator by Lorne, James and

Matt took the elevator down to the parking garage. Lorne is a young man of twenty-two years old he's a computer genius that got cot six years back hacking into the JBI's main computer, after that he was put on twenty-four hour house watch he wasn't allowed to use or be around computers for a year. After he was taken off house watch the JBI hired him as their Technical Analysis. "Oh hi Lorne" Hayden said "can I talk with you for a second" Lorne asked him "sure" Hayden replied, they went to Lorne's office "what can I do for you Lorne" Hayden said to him "I heard the Director on the phone talking about budget cuts and the staff at the Behavioral Science Division (BSD) I guess what I'm trying to say or ask is if the team is getting separated" Lorne asked "not that I know of" Hayden replied and continued "and don't worry about budget cuts they've been talking about budget cuts for the past ten years" Hayden assured him "so the teams not breaking up" Lorne asked for clarity "no" Hayden told him "thank God" Lorne said as he smiled and hugged Hayden. Hayden was use to Lorne's cheerful and bubbly personality but not with the open display of affection "no hugging Lorne" he said "I'm sorry no hugging" Lorne apologized as he released Hayden.

Matt went with James in James black Escalade to the Big Ticket Movie theater near Tilliquimsara Beach. "So I heard you scored five hundred on your firearms test" James said to Matt "yeah I'm a surgeon with this handgun" Matt replied jokingly "not bad kid but don't let it get to your head in two months your up for a review, an opportunity to move up to Senior Profiler" James told him "I'm well aware of that" Matt said "it won't be easy" James informed him "how long were you with the bureau before you got to Senior Profiler" Matt asked James "six years" James replied. "I've only been here four years" Matt said "you've excelled at your work quicker than I ever did" James told him "really you think so" Matt asked flattered from what James said, James gave him a smile "just try not to lose focus" James told him. They weren't too far from the BTM "we're almost there, next couple lights make a left" Matt said "you ever watched a movie at a BTM" Matt asked James "maybe back in high school not recently though" James replied "I heard they're much cheaper than the regular theater" Matt said "well if they're playing movies like Purple Noon they better be" James said sarcastically. James made a left turn at the next traffic light, he entered into a gated parking lot that belonged to the BTM and parked his Escalade. They got out of the vehicle and headed up the steps that were in front of the theater "who do we ask for when we get inside" Matt asked "the general manager" James replied. James pushed open the BTM's front door and they went inside, inside the BTM the floor was carpeted, to their left was a series of ticket counters and to their right were two concession stands that sold popcorn, drinks, nachos and various types of candies. James and Matt went to a ticket counter that a young lady wearing a BTM t-shirt was standing behind "hi my name is James Morris from the JBI this is my partner Matt Davis we're working a case right now we'd like to ask you a couple questions" he said to the lady as he showed her his badge "okay" she replied. "Were you working last night" James asked her "yes I was covering a shift for a friend" she replied, James took out the picture of Dee-dee Simmons from his shirt pocket and showed it to her "have you seen this lady" he asked her "I'm not sure she looks like the lady that was speaking with Andy" she told James "Andy" James asked "yeah he was working at one of the ticket counters last night" she replied "is he here now" Matt inquired "no he's off today" she told him. "Is there anything else you remember about her" James asked the young lady "yeah I remember she wasn't alone" she said "who was she with" James asked her "she came with another lady" she replied. James looked at Matt as Matt was writing down what the young lady was telling them on a piece of paper, James looked back at the young lady "what's your name mam" he asked her "Allison" she replied "is that all Allison" he said to her "that's all I remember" Allison told them. "We're going to need the name of the friend she came here with" Matt told her "okay her name is Beth Unger" Allison replied "you know her last name" James asked Allison thinking that was strange "yeah I know her from before, she use to come here every Saturday and she recently just stopped, she was one of our regular customers, nice lady" Allison replied "she lives in Palmbrook" she added. James knew he had some good information and a good lead "thank you for your time mam" he said to Allison and shook her hand.

Hayden was on Highway 33 heading into Amaryllis Jaiz to check out Slaps Bed & Breakfast. Amaryllis Jaiz was about a half an hour west of Brookshore it was a city people went to, to take pictures and couples went to, to get married, its nickname is the City Of Flowers. Its a very beautiful city with rolling hills in its northwestern section, from Highway 33 you can see various types of flowers growing on its plush green lawns, the southeastern section of it faces the pristine water of Hubber's Lake. Ravi saw the sign that said 'Welcome To Amaryllis Jaiz' so he exited off the highway onto Route 11 that took them into the city. Earlier Lorne had e-mailed the address for Slaps to Hayden's cell-phone, it was located at 114, east Route 9, Ravi had it programmed in the GPS device in the car so he knew that they were getting close. Ravi made a right turn on Route 30 then a left on Route 9, when he got onto Route

9 he started looking out for the address and so did Hayden. They didn't have to go too far east from the intersection of Route 30 when Hayden spotted the building "there it is" he said to Ravi, Ravi stopped and parked the car in front of the building. Slaps Bed & Breakfast is a two story mansion built of raw stone with green ivy vines covering most of the building the top of it was built of red concrete shingles shaped like bamboo on its windowsills hang wooden planters that displayed various tropical flowers, there was a steel gate surrounding the mansion. Hayden got out of the car and went up to the front passenger door, he asked Ravi to roll down the window and he obliged "this might take awhile so feel free to grab something to eat" he told Ravi and headed up to the gate. There was a buzzer button on a small metal panel with a speaker-phone beside it mounted on the gate, he pushed the buzzer and the gate automatically opened. Hayden went for a short walk up to the front door, when he got to the front door he pushed it open and went in, inside Slaps was carpeted with carpet that had a paisley design and is royal-purple in color, on the walls hung classical paintings of women and boats. Hayden went up to the front desk that was to his left, a young lady wearing a short black dress and high-heel shoes was sitting behind the desk "hi welcome to Slaps Bed & Breakfast do you have a room booked" she asked Hayden, Hayden showed

her his JBI identification "I'm here to see a Madam Zebandee" he told the lady "one second I'll buzz her right now" the lady replied with a smile "thank you" Hayden said to her as he stood there and waited for the madam. To Hayden Slaps looked like a brothel with scantily clad young women walking around, there was also young men in their twenties to early thirties walking around only wearing white t-shirts and sneakers, very athletic looking young men that had black satin mask on their face. Madam Zebandee opened the door to a room beside the front desk she was with a young man, when they came out to the lobby where Hayden was she gave him a slap on his bare butt and he headed down the hall to a staircase leading upstairs. She extended her hand out to Hayden "hi I'm Madam Zebandee" she said, Hayden shook her hand "Special Agent Hayden Alexander" he replied "how can I help you Hayden" she asked him "I'm working a case in Brookshore that has brought me here, do you know this lady" Hayden asked her as he showed her a picture of Dee-dee Simmons "yes she's a cook here" Madam Zebandee replied. Madam Zebandee was a chubby lady in her late fifties she was wearing a pearl-white chieftain dress with pockets and a silver silk scarf wrapped around her head covering her long black hair, on her feet she wore earth-tone sandals. "Is she in some kind of trouble" she asked "her body was discovered this morning" Hayden informed her "oh my god" she said as she covered her mouth in disbelief "do you know if she had any enemies" Hayden asked her. "No she was very quiet always to herself, she did have a friend Beth she is also a cook here" Madam Zebandee replied "do you mind if we go out back I really need a cigarette" she asked Hayden "sure" Hayden replied as he allowed her to lead the way. He followed her through the mansion to the backyard, on their way there they walked by a large living room where young naked women in high heel shoes were laying on their stomachs on a couch watching a big screen TV, some were laying on a white alpaca rug. The hallway they were walking down was decorated with stone statues of naked men, there was the sound of soft jazz music coming through the mansion's speaker system. Madam Zebandee opened a sliding-door to the backyard, as they entered into the backyard to Hayden it was like walking into a garden the grass was plush green and neatly trimmed it was filled with various tropical flowers and plants there was an in-ground swimming pool, around the swimming pool young men and women were laying on towels sunbathing in the nude, Madam Zebandee closed back the door. She reached in her pocket and pulled out a pack of cigarettes, she took one out of the pack and lit it with a silver Zippo lighter she had in her other pocket and then put the pack back in her pocket, she inhaled two puffs of smoke and then exhaled. "Where did you find her" she asked Hayden "in a vacant lot near the BTM at Tilliquimsara Beach" Hayden replied "yeah she told me that her and Beth was going to watch a movie there" Madam Zebandee said "does Dee-dee have any family" Hayden asked her "yeah her parents they live in Brookshore" she replied as she took a couple more puffs of her cigarette "did Dee-dee live with them" he inquired "no her and her boyfriend rented an apartment here in Amaryllis Jaiz until he died of cancer so now she was living there alone" Madam Zebandee replied. Madam Zebandee outed the butt of her cigarette in an ashtray that was on a small table beside her "how long has she been working here" Hayden asked her "she got hired just after her boyfriend died so its been around two years" she replied "did she mention any guy she was seeing or occasionally dating" Hayden asked her "no Dee-dee was true to her boyfriend he was the love of her life" Madam Zebandee replied as she lit up another cigarette "I'm going to need her address here in Amaryllis Jaiz and also her parents address in Brookshore" Hayden said to her "I have all that information in my office" she told Hayden. After Madam Zebandee finished her second cigarette they went to her office and she gave Hayden Dee-dee's information "all her information is in this folder and here's her pay cheque to, when you see her parents can you give them that for me" she said to Hayden referring to the cheque as she handed him the folder and the cheque. Hayden took a business card out of his pocket "if there is anything you remember that you forgot to tell me please don't hesitate to call me" Hayden said to her as he handed her his card.

James and Matt headed out to Palmbrook to find Beth. Matt called Lorne on his cell-phone and asked him to find the address for a Beth Unger "where does she live" Lorne asked Matt "Palmbrook" Matt replied "okay I'll send you the information in five minutes" Lorne told him. "What's the quickest way to get there" Matt asked James as he hung up his phone "if we take Harrington Drive we should be there in fifteen minutes" James replied. James turned off the PBP onto Harrington Drive that headed northwest out of downtown Brookshore "so Allison is quite the looker eh" Matt said to James "keep focus" James told him. James looked at Matt's phone "did you get the address" James asked him, Matt looked at his phone "yeah it's 417 Cyrilla Lane" Matt replied, James typed it in the GPS. "The GPS says we're eleven minutes away" James told Matt, Matt took out a pen and pad from his jacket pocket and started writing down a list of questions he was going to ask Beth.

Ann Miller stepped off the number five bus onto Jaden Street, she didn't live too far from the bus stop. She headed south down Jaden Street past a row of gift shops, it was now 8:00pm, she usually got a lift home after her shift at the office, she was a secretary for a law firm. After the row of shops she was now walking by Castle Park a fare size park that had trees and bushes in it, Ann was just a half a block away from where she lives. She opened her purse to get her keys just then someone bull-rushed her from the left side, punching her in the jaw knocking her out, he then dragged her unconscious body into the park.

The next morning around 9am Ann's body was found by a city parks worker in a cluster of Dwarf Allamanda shrubs, the body was nude with contusions on her head and a large abrasion on her throat, it also had seventeen stab wounds to the torso. The police and coroner's showed up after the distrot parks worker called 661 emergency, the ambulance came soon after and took the parks worker to their van. Chief of police Major Byron Phelps was standing next to the body talking to a officer as a couple other officers taped off the crime scene "I guess we should call the feds" he said to the officer. Byron took Hayden's card out of the breast pocket of his shirt and called him on his cell phone "hi it's Chief Phelps you better get out here we got another one" he informed Hayden "I'm at Jaden just two block south of Kessler's Market" Byron told him and hung up. "Looks like we got a psycho in town" Byron said to the officer beside him "yes sir" the officer replied, the coroner covered the body with a white blanket. It took Hayden just under ten minutes to get to the crime scene he had just gotten back from having dinner in Amaryllis Jaiz at a Ghanaian restaurant last night with Ravi, James and Matt showed up after. "So what do we have chief" Hayden asked Byron as he stood over the body "a city parks worker found her forty minutes ago while pruning the bushes" Byron told him as he took the blanket from off the body. Hayden stooped down to get a better look at the body "looks like he broke her jaw" he said to Byron "yeah I saw that" Byron replied. Earlier on the coroner had handed Byron a I.D card that he had found in the bushes near the body so Byron gave it to Hayden "we found this I.D card near the body" he told Hayden as he handed it to him. Hayden looked at it "Ann Miller born November 20th, 1984" he said to himself just then he saw at the corner of his eye sticking out from under the body's right leg a match-book baring the name Slaps Bed & Breakfast. He took it and gave it to an officer "can you put this in a evidence-bag for me" he said to the officer, Hayden could also see that there were black metal specks around the body's vaginal area, same as Dee-dee's body. Hayden knew that Ann was killed by the same person that killed Dee-dee and there was a connection with Slaps.

Two days ago Ann and her friend Mariam a paralegal at the law firm she worked at were at Slaps Bed & Breakfast celebrating Mariam's engagement

M C WILLIAMS

to her long time boyfriend. After Hayden finished collecting evidence the coroner took the body, Hayden knew he had to go back to Slaps.

James and Matt walked up to Hayden "looks like this is the work of the same person that killed Dee-dee" James said "yes the pattern's the same" Hayden replied "we just got back from Palmbrook, from seeing Beth Unger" Matt told Hayden. "What did you find out" Hayden asked Matt "well Beth works at Slaps Bed& Breakfast along with Dee-dee and two nights before Dee-dee was murdered both Beth and Dee-dee were being harassed by a man named Terry he was a guess there" Matt replied. "Okay this is what I want you to do, I sent a match-book back to the lab to get checked for fingerprints, you two get back there as soon as possible and also let Lorne know to get me some information on Slaps Bed & Breakfast and a Madam Zebandee" Hayden instructed James and Matt "we'll get right on it" James told him.

After Hayden collected all the evidence that he needed from the scene he headed down the street to where he seen Ravi was parked. Ravi was parked in front of a sub-sandwich shop next to Kessler Market, he was in the car checking messages on his phone mostly from family members checking up on him like his sister in Tamerra. Hayden got back to the car and went over to the driver's side window which was open "hey" Hayden said trying to scare Ravi but

24

failed "oh you're finished, that was quick" Ravi said as he turned his head to face Hayden "we're going back to Slaps Bed & Breakfast" Hayden told him "okay" Ravi said and then put his phone back in its cradle that was mounted on the dashboard. As Ravi started up the car Hayden checked for any messages on his cell-phone, after seeing that he had no new messages he decided on calling Lorne. "Hello Oracle Lorne at your service" he answered with a humorous voice "hi Lorne it's Hayden" Hayden said "hi sir how can I help you" Lorne asked him in his normal voice "I need an information and ID check on a Madam Zebandee the owner of Slaps Bed & Breakfast" he told Lorne "okay I'll get it to you in five minutes" Lorne replied "thank you" Hayden said and hung up the phone.

(Embedded Narrative)
GARNET RIDGE POINT

In Tamerra things were quieting down after what happened in the Black Forest and at the Space Lab a year ago, the tension Moses felt with the Janoesian Army hunting him had stopped do to the incarceration of Terrance Banes formally known as General Banes, Terrance was stripped of whatever metals and stripes he achieved throughout his military career, Moses was able to enjoy some time with Stacey. He had bought a ring for Stacey and decided on taking her out to Garnet Ridge Point to give it to her. Moses parked his truck at the point, they both get out and sit on the hood of his truck "such a nice night" Stacey said looking up at the clear dark sky decorated in constellations, Moses held her hand and turned and faced her "I guess there's no time like the present" Moses said to himself. "What's this about" Stacey asked him curious to know, Moses gives her the ring "I want to be with you for the rest of my life, this is a promise ring symbolizing that I'll never leave you" Moses told her and putted it on her finger. Stacey smiled admiring the ring and gave Moses a hug "thank you" she said to him and kissed him. Stacey sat on Moses lap, she was wearing a purple thong bikini bottom and a thin white knitted sweater that was long enough in the back to cover up her bottom. They stared out at the midnight-blue Atlantic, she turns and smiles at him and kisses her hero again and he excepts her grace and affection so he holds her tight in his well toned arms as he listens to her let out a delightful gasp of joy. The next day they woke up realizing that they slept overnight at the point, they got off the hood of Moses truck and went in the truck's cab "I guess we lost track of time" Stacey said "yeah no worries though, are you hungry" Moses asked her "yes a little" Stacey replied. Moses knew of a great roti place down at the bottom of the point, he started up his F-150 and drove down there, Stacey sat in the passenger seat tying an elastic-band around her hair, putting it in a ponytail "do you think they'll be open yet" she asked Moses "not sure, doesn't hurt to find out though" he replied as he turned into the shop's parking lot. The shop's neon sign was blinking but it didn't look like the shop was open, "wait here" Moses told Stacey, he exited the truck and went over to the shop's front door to see what time they open, there was a six days a week time of service posted on the front door. Moses could see that today they opened up at 10:00am, he checked his watch, it was only 8:25am, he went back to the truck. "So when do they open" Stacey asked as Moses got in the truck and closed the door "we have an hour and a half to wait" Moses informed her "I guess we wait then" Stacey said "or we could look elsewhere" Moses suggests. Stacey really liked it at the point and didn't mind waiting till the roti shop opened "I guess they open up later in the off season" Moses said as he turned on the radio, surfing through the channels looking for a news station "can we not listen to the radio right now" Stacey asked him "what else is there to do, there's nobody around even to speak to" he told her "sure there is" Stacey said and took off her sweater revealing her round supple breast. Moses looked at her "round two" he asked her, she gave him a lustful smile that's when he held her in his arms and started kissing her face and neck as he laid her down on the seat in the cab, he slowly moved his hands down to her waist and took off her bikini-bottom. After they made love they got dress and went for a walk down to the water, as they walked Stacey was cuddled up next to her hero with both her arms around his muscular arm "do you think the president will keep your secret" she asked Moses. Moses looked down at her and smiled "yeah I do, I trust him" he replied, they kissed each other "the only thing is that it's too bad that we had to deport Jessepi back to Cuba" Moses said "it's good though that he's not allowed back in this country" Stacey added. Before they stepped on the sand Moses took off his sandals and rolled up the foot of his blue-jeans, he gave Stacey a slap on the butt and ran for the water, Stacey let out a giggly scream as she felt the sweet-sting of the slap and ran after Moses "oh I'm gonna get you" she told him. They started to play-fight in the knee high water, Moses lifted up Stacey and threw her in the water, she splashed about and then stood up and used her hands to splash water on Moses "you like that" she asked Moses as she splashed him. Moses waded in the water awhile an got out and him and Stacey sat on the sand allowing the morning sun to dry them off "that felt nice" he said to Stacey "yeah we needed that after sitting in that warm truck" Stacey replied. It didn't take them long to dry off, they sat there staring at the crystal-blue water, people started to arrive at the beach, young couples with their babies and teenagers looking to catch that early morning surf. Moses looked at his watch, it was 9:20am "lets go" he said to Stacey, they got up and went back to his truck to wait for the roti shop to open. Moses sat in the truck fishing through its glove-compartment looking for a can of Blue Toucan he thought he left in there, but there was nothing in there "SHIT!" he said out loud "what is it" Stacey asked him "I thought I had a can of beer in here" He replied. Stacey put her hand on Moses shoulder "don't worry the beer stores are almost open" she assured him. Moses turned on the radio to a contemporary music station, he started drinking the bottled water he brought with him, twenty-five minutes had already gone by and it was now 9:45am, Stacey could see the owner opening up the service-window to the roti shop. "Hey look they're opening up" she said to Moses as she pointed at the shop "no they're not open yet not for another fifteen minutes" Moses told her. Moses watched as a young couple in their late teens to early twenties walked up to the roti shop and sat on one of the benches that were in front of the shop, the girl was wearing a g-string bikini, from the back to Moses it didn't look like she had any bottoms on, her round plump bottom bounced as Moses watched them walk to the bench, another couple sitting under a cabana close by also noticed the young girl's sexy bottom. Fifteen minutes went by and it was now 10:00am, Moses and Stacey got out of the truck and went up to the roti shop where a small line was accumulating. They stood in line waiting to be served "what are you thinking of getting" Stacey asked Moses "I was thinking of the boneless goat roti" Moses replied, Moses realized that they were standing behind the young couple, the girl had tied a powdered-blue silk see-through scarf around her waist that covered her bottom. The line went quick and it was now Moses and Stacey's turn, Moses ordered the boneless goat roti and Stacey, she wasn't that hungry so she ordered a banana split. Moses paid for their orders and they went back to his truck, they sat in the truck eating their food "do you think that's the last we seen of Jessepi" Stacey suddenly asked Moses "I don't know it's hard to say" Moses replied "why do you ask" he said to Stacey "no reason, it's just, from what I heard he seems well connected in Cuba" she replied "I doubt it, at the airport his passport was stamped with a Janoesian Ban, he's not allowed back in the country" Moses assured her. They finished up their food and put the empty containers on the back seat of the cab, Moses started up the truck "so where do you want to go, back up to the point" he asked Stacey "I feel like walking along the boardwalk at AquaHorn" she replied. Moses entered onto Route 55 going south, it was only a five minute drive to the boardwalk depending on traffic. Moses had a pretty good idea what Stacey wanted to do when they got there, Stacey liked to window-shop as she walked on the boardwalk, looking in the display windows of the gift-shops that lined the boardwalk. Moses pulled into an empty parking spot in front of a gift-shop "here we are" he said to Stacey as he put the truck in park, Stacey got out of the truck, Moses also got out of the truck and went around to Stacey's side. Moses held her hand as he came up beside her and they walked to the boardwalk. The beach wasn't too busy but it was busy enough for being the off-season, the only people populating it were adults and retirees all the kids were back in school. Moses liked this time of year it meant he didn't have to wait in long lines and there was always room on the beach for him to sit, he actually liked walking on the boardwalk especially with Stacey "so are you going to buy something this time" he asked Stacey as he held her close noticing that she was looking at a gift-shop "I bought something the last time we were here" she replied in a sweet subtle voice with a little wine in her tone "I don't remember you buying anything" Moses said with a chuckle. He held her in his arms close as they went for a stroll down the boardwalk, Stacey enjoyed having Moses back as his normal self but she knew that an incident might take place that will cause the transformation. "I hope they can find a cure soon" she said to Moses, he knew exactly what she was talking about "I thought we agreed that I would keep this gift" he asked Stacey "I know, I just worry that you won't change back from the transformation" she replied softly as she rubbed his muscular chest with the palm of her hand "don't worry hon I'll always be here right beside you" Moses assured her and then gave her a love-pat and squeeze on the bottom, Stacey let out a gasp and they hugged and kissed on the boardwalk.

HOT ON THE TRAIL

While Ravi headed down Highway 33 to Amaryllis Jaiz Lorne called back Hayden with some information on Madam Zebandee. "Hi sir, I got that information you were looking for" Lorne told Hayden "okay" Hayden replied as he waited for Lorne to give him the straight-skinny on Madam Zebandee. Lorne read from the information that was on his computer screen "Delmira Gosslett aka Madam Zebandee born July 3rd, 1960 in Umni, Janoesha Harbour, she studied sociology at a college in Alan's Landing and four years after she graduated she was arrested for credit card fraud in 1988 at the age of twenty-seven, she spent two years in jail for that offense, in 1994 she won the Top Spin Lottery in Alan's Landing, the payout for it was $5 million, after that in 1995 she bought that estate in Amaryllis Jaiz and six months later she opened up Slaps Bed & breakfast" Lorne informed Hayden. "thank you Lorne" Hayden said "oh one more thing" Lorne said "she has a younger brother that lives here in Brookshore, he works as a diesel mechanic for Outland Logistics his name is Ronald Gosslett" Lorne added "thank you" Hayden said and then hung-up the phone.

James and Matt were back at the crime lab waiting as they watched CSI super-glue a matchbook for fingerprints that was sent their by Hayden from the Ann Miller crime scene. After the super-gluing was done they brought the matchbook over to a computer and looked for a match in AFIS on a print they lifted off the matchbook. They found a match to an unsolved rape and murder from 1993, it was the rape and murder of nineteen year old Julie Castorac, the file was sent to the Cold Case Division. Julie Castorac's body was found in some bushes near Mollymawk Marina, her jaw was broken and they found black metal specks around her vaginal area like she had been penetrated with a metal object. "Does it say if a metal object was found at the scene" James asked the CSI agent "no nothing like that was found" the agent replied "that means whatever he used he brought with him" James said.

When they arrived at Slaps Bed & Breakfast Madam Zebandee was out in the backyard spanking a young man for taking something out of one of the girls purse without asking. The young man was bent over her knee as she spanked his bare bottom, he was wriggling and screaming as his soft round cheeks danced in pain under Madam Zebandee's hand "this will teach you not to take what doesn't belong to you" she told him as she continued spanking his bottom. Most of the girls that worked there were crowded around Madam Zebandee watching the young man get spanked, some were giggling others were watching in aw and shock feeling sorry for the young man. The receptionist came to the backyard to let Madam Zebandee know that there was someone here to see her. Madam Zebandee finished up spanking the young man, he got up from over her lap, sobbing in tears sorry for his defiants, he immediately started rubbing his sore bottom as the girls around him sneaked a feel, caressing his round bubble-butt as he tried to keep away their hands from touching him, giggling at his shame as they gently squeezed. Madam Zebandee got up out of the lawn-chair she was sitting in and hugged him "no more stealing okay" she told him and continued "go and get some Nivea rubbed on that" she told him and gave him one final slap on his bottom as he walked away clutching the hem of his small white t-shirt trying to cover his genitals.

Hayden was in the lobby waiting for Madam Zebandee, the receptionist came back to let him know that Madam Zebandee was coming. Hayden noticed that it wasn't the same receptionist working when he came here the last time, he watched her as she sat down behind the front desk. When she turned her head to look at him he immediately turned away and pretended to be looking at the paintings on the wall. The receptionist was an attractive lady she looked to be in her mid-thirties, she sat behind the desk staring at Hayden admiring his debonaire style, she looked him up and down as he stared at the painting on the wall, Hayden was wearing a grey slim fit cotton dress pants and a pink contemporary fit dress shirt, on his feet he was wearing a pare of black Elkan Cap-Toe Oxfords, he also wore a grey Trilby on his head that he was now holding in his hand. "We don't get much police around here" she said to Hayden "how did you know" Hayden asked her as he turned around to face her "your badge is sticking out of your shirt-pocket" she replied "oh right" Hayden said as he tucked his badge back in his shirt-pocket. Hayden thought that maybe this lady knew something that could help him in the case "how long have you been working here" he asked the lady "about three years" she replied, Hayden showed her a picture of Ann Miller "have

37

you seen this lady in here" he asked her "yeah she looks like the lady that was here three nights ago with a couple friends, it looked like they were celebrating some kind of promotion or an accomplishment in sales" she replied "was she talking to anyone else other than the women she came there with" Hayden inquired "no not really but there is one thing, when they were in the lounge drinking there was a man at the other end of the bar that was staring at her, I mean really gunning her down" she replied "can you describe this man" Hayden asked her "it's hard to say the lights were dimmed, he looked to be about six feet tall with short brown hair, sorry that's all I can remember" she said to Hayden "was there anything that stood out about him" Hayden asked digging for more information "no he looked like a regular guy, oh yeah he wore glasses with thick dark rims" she replied. Hayden put the picture of Ann Miller back in his pants pocket "thank you mam for your time" he said to the lady "please call me Rose, mam makes me sound old" she said as she gave him a smile. Hayden took a business card out of his shirt-pocket "Rose if there's anything else you can remember about that night don't hesitate to call me" Hayden told her as he handed her his card. Rose looked at his card "JBI very impressive" she said, Hayden gave her a controlled-smile as he called James on his cell-phone "excuse me" Hayden said to Rose and walked away from her desk. James answered on the other end "hi James how's it going at the lab" he asked James "very well, they lifted a print off the matchbook it matched an unsolved case from 1993, the rape and murder of Julie Castorac" James replied "I remember that case from back in university" Hayden said "get this, black metal specks were also found around her vaginal area" James added. "Sounds good James, I have something else for you and Matt to look into" Hayden told him "that's what I'm here for" James replied "Madam Zebandee has a younger brother he's local in Brookshore, he works as a diesel mechanic for Outland Logistics, his name is Ronald Gosslett, I want you to go over there and find out if he has any information about Slaps Bed & Breakfast" Hayden told him "sure thing" James replied "but before you do, get Lorne to run his name for warrants" Hayden said "will do" James replied, Hayden hung up the phone. Just then Madam Zebandee came into the front lobby "hello agent" she said to Hayden "you came back, are you here for business or pleasure" she asked him "strictly business mam" Hayden replied. "That's too bad" Madam Zebandee said "the reason why I came back is because I found a matchbook from here at one of my crime scenes" Hayden told her "I don't know anything about that, thousands of people stay here each mouth, it could be anyone in Amaryllis Jaiz that had that matchbook" she explained to Hayden. Hayden looked at her not too sure if he should believe her "would it be okay for me to do a search of the building" he asked Madam Zebandee just to see what she would say "I guess so, it would have to be later on this evening, what are you looking for" she asked him with a concerned voice "it's just something we do to rule you out as a suspect" Hayden replied "I'm going to have two uniformed officers posted here in the lobby until I come back with a warrant" he informed Madam Zebandee "I'll be here" she told him.

James and Matt left the JBI lab and headed out to Outland Logistics, Matt had done a Google search for it online and found an address. It was located at 50 Doral Circle which was just east of Highway 34 close to the Brookend overpass. Matt typed the address in the vehicles GPS "you know that address looks familiar, I think I've been there before" James said to Matt "are you sure" Matt asked "yeah if it's the same place they ship barrels there" James replied "well we'll soon find out" Matt said. "So what did Lorne say when you gave him Ronald's name" Matt asked James "Lorne's research-log is backed up, an influx of unsolved cases, but he said he'll get back to me in twenty minutes" James informed him "there's that much unsolved cases" Matt asked in unbelief "yeah it's actually cases spread throughout Passco Region" James replied "okay so it's not just in Brookshore, well that makes sense" Matt said relieved to hear his city wasn't becoming a haven for criminals. James exited off the highway onto Silvercreek Road heading west, Silvercreek Road was a main road that headed into downtown Brookshore going west. They didn't have to travel too far to find Doral Circle, when they got there they saw that it was a culdesac with four corporate buildings, Outland Logistics was on the northwest corner of Silvercreek Road & Doral Circle. James drove the black Escalade up the driveway of Outland Logistics and parked it in their spacious parking lot around back. James and Matt got out of the vehicle and walked around the building to the front door, James pushed the door open and they stepped into the front lobby. There was a young lady wearing a headset sitting behind a desk, James and Matt both walked up to the desk, James flashed his JBI I.D at the lady "hi we're here to see Ronald Gosslett" James told her. "He's on break right now, I'll call for him" the young lady said to James, she got on the intercom and ask for Ronald Gosslett to come to the front lobby "it should only take him a few minutes to get here" she told James and Matt "thank you" James said to her. Just then James cell-phone rang, it was Lorne "hey Lorne, you got anything for me" James asked Lorne "not really Ronald Edward Gosslett has a clean record, the only trouble he got into was back when he was eighteen, him and a friend of his got cot in a stolen car, it turns out that Ronald didn't have nothing to do with it, his friend at the time told him that it was his mother's car so all charges were dropped and it was expunged from his record" Lorne informed James "thank you" James said "not a problem" Lorne replied and hung up the phone. James put his phone back in his pocket "what did he say" Matt asked him "he said Ronald has a clean record" James replied "well that helps his cause" Matt said sarcastically. Ronald entered in the lobby from a door behind the front desk, he was wearing blue-jeans, a white t-shirt with a black leather apron over it, on his feet he had on work-boots. He walked over to where James and Matt were standing "hi you want to see me" Ronald said to James and Matt "we're here about your sister" James told him "my sister, I haven't seen her in five years" Ronald replied, confuse to what was going on. "There has been two murders that both lead back to where she works, we know she didn't do them but she may know who did, we're here to ask you if you know any of the people she acquaints herself with" James explained to him "no I'm sorry we hardly talk to each other, we had a fallen-out about fifteen years ago" Ronald told him "where did you guys meet five years ago" Matt asked Ronald "at a family reunion" Ronald replied "where was it at" James inquired "Hubber's Lake Park" Ronald answered "do I need a lawyer" Ronald asked the two men, concerned about his rights "no you're not in any trouble" Matt assured him.

Grand Mall is located in downtown Brookshore among office buildings, corporate high-rises and street-side plazas. In the food court at the mall Terry sat around a table eating a two piece chicken dinner with fries out of a cardboard container labeled St. Hubert Chicken. He sat there dipping his fries into a glob of ketchup he had poured onto a clear spot in the container, he was watching women not just any women, young attractive business women, ones that work at the office, that commute on the InnerHoop. He picked up the bottle of Sprite he had bought with the chicken dinner and started drinking, washing down the remainder of the fries he had eating. For Terry this was a regular day, he would routinely hangout at the mall, it was either this or Mollymawk Marina, more women came to the mall than the marina, he would have went to Tilliquimsara Beach but there's too many cops there. Terry got up from around the table and threw the empty container and bottle in one of the garbage-cans in the food-court. He started following a group of young executive women that just finished being on their lunch break and were heading back to the office, he kept a safe distance away as not to raise anyone's suspicions, Terry's outer appearance didn't hurt him either, with his short brown hair and subtle facial features. He was wearing a light-blue button-up shirt and tanned-khaki Levi pants on his feet he wore blue Converse sneakers, he's a very approachable person when you first meet him. Terry strolled through the mall's hallway behind the group of women, he was fixated on a specific one, she was the branch manager for RL Home Outfitters right here in Brookshore. She was Terry's type, long dark hair, five feet seven inches tall with an athletic built, no Terry wasn't going to let this one go, the group of women split up as they left the mall through a set of swinging doors leading outside, Terry kept following the one he was interested in, she was the only one in the group that didn't go through the swinging doors. He followed her to the mall's underground parking, Terry wasn't going to take her life just yet he just wanted to see what type of vehicle she drove and then follow her to see where she worked.

Dana Hollinger is a thirty-five year old Branch Manager for RL Home Outfitters in southeast Brookshore, she had come to the mall to meet some friends on her lunch break. I guess the feeling started when she was sitting around a table in the food-court eating lunch with her friends, for some strange reason she felt like the man in the light-blue shirt sitting alone to her left four tables over was watching them, and not just watching them but stalking them. The group of women finished their lunches and left the food-court, Dana noticed that not long after they left the man in the light-blue shirt got up and followed behind them, this raised Dana's concerns but she didn't want to alarm the group of women she was with so she just continued walking, waiting to see if the man would turn and go in another direction but he never did. It also could be that her feeling was wrong and he wasn't stalking them 'it's not like he was right behind them' Dana thought to herself. The ladies went their separate ways at a set of swinging doors leading outside, Dana headed to the mall's underground parking, beside the door leading to the underground parking was a mirror the same height as the door but only three inches wide. As Dana opened the door leading out to underground parking she could see through the mirror the man in the light-blue shirt standing by a flower store watching her, this creeped out Dana, as she got into underground parking she slammed the door behind her and ran to where her car was parked, fishing for her keys as she got closer to her car, she found them and opened the car door, she got in and slammed the door shut. Dana was so scared that she was sitting there inside her car trying to calm herself down, it took her a few seconds to get her breathing back to normal and calm down, she positioned the rear-view mirror above the car's dashboard and took a look through it before she put the key in the ignition. Through the rear-view mirror she saw the same man in the light-blue shirt standing inside the door of the underground parking still staring at her, now with a creepy smirk on his face, Dana started up the car and backed out of the parking space, she accelerated the car to the exit of the underground parking and then out onto the streets of downtown Brookshore.

Terry stood near a flower shop and watched as the young lady entered into underground parking. He then made his way into the underground parking and saw her get into a red 2012 Pontiac Sunfire, the car sped off through the underground parking exit. Terry ran and got into his 1979 Mustang L, he started it up and gave chase, he followed the red Sunfire going east on Silvercreek Road. Terry wasn't far behind her, he swerved in and out of traffic to keep her in his sight plus his car was souped up with a custom built engine that has a nitrous oxide system in it. Terry was now just two cars behind his prey and that's where he stayed as he tailed her, Terry followed her to the corporate building of RL Home Outfitters in southeast Brookshore. There was a security gate at the entrance, he parked his car a block away under a Avocado tree and watched as the security gate opened up for the red Sunfire, Terry wrote down the address on a notepad he had on the dash of his car. He knew this would be his next victim, he sat there planning a strategy of attack in his head, he then looked down at the floor under the front passenger seat at a black-steel pipe stuffed with rubber, at one end a brown rubber ball was attached the other end was wrapped with black electrical tape, Terry smiled to himself as he looked at the pipe.

Hayden came back later in the evening to Slaps Bed & Breakfast with a search warrant and six JBI agents, the warrant was only to search Madam Zebandee's office and the lounge. Hayden gave Madam Zebandee the warrant as him and the agents entered in the front door "this is for you Madam" he said, she took the warrant, "please don't break anything" she begged the agents as three of them headed for the lounge. Hayden and the other three agents went into Madam Zebandee's office and shut the door behind them, two uniformed officers were still standing post in the lobby, Madam Zebandee went into the living room to lay down on the couch. Hayden and one agent went through Madam Zebandee's desk, they were looking for anyone linked to Dee-dee or Ann Miller, the other two agents were rifling through her filing cabinets. They were at it for over three hours, reading through file after file of useless information, they were getting nowhere, Hayden had hit a dead-end here, at least so he thought until one of the agents in the lounge called him over to watch a recording of one of the security-cameras. "Keep looking" Hayden told the agents as he left and went to the lounge, when he got there one of the agents escorted his to a security-booth behind the bar. In there Hayden watched on a group of monitors a man sitting at the bar apparently stalking a young lady sitting at a table, Hayden watched as the lady got up from around the table and left the lounge, about a minute after the man followed behind her. The agent watched as the man came closer to the camera and then paused the image "this was recorded five days ago" the agent told Hayden "okay get that tape to the lab and have them try to make an identification on the man in the recording, good work" Hayden told the agent. 'Maybe Madam Zebandee knows who he is' Hayden then thought to himself "hold on one second" Hayden told the agents "I'm going to have Madam Zebandee take a look at the video" he informed them. An agent went to get Madam Zebandee, she was still in the living room laying on the couch reading a magazine, the young agent entered into the living room "mam they want to see you in the lounge" he informed Madam Zebandee. She got up out of the couch and rested the magazine on the crystal-center-piece that was in front of the couch, the agent walked with her back to the lounge. They went into the security booth, Hayden was in there with another agent "hi Madam, I want you to take a look at a video and tell if you recognized the person in the video" Hayden said to her. She sat down in front of the group of monitors, an agent played the tape for her, she watched as the tape ran for five minutes, the agent paused it "do you recognize the man at the bar" Hayden asked her "yeah that's T, he comes in here once in a while" Madam Zebandee replied "do you have an actual name for him" Hayden inquired "no just T, all his receipts are signed T" she informed him. "Do you know what kind of car he drives" Hayden asked her, pressing for information he could work with "I believe it's a dark colored Mustang early eighties model" she replied "are you sure" Hayden asked her "yes, if not you can check for yourself, all parking cards are filed in a docket that I keep in the top drawer of my desk" she told him. "Okay wait here I'll be back" Hayden told Madam Zebandee, he had the agents stay with her as he went back to her office to check the top drawer of her desk.

James and Matt just got back to the JBI building from Outland Logistics "I can't see not speaking to my sister for years" Matt said to James as they took the elevator up to the Behavioral Science floor "some families are bound by blood and not love" James told him "well it just seems strange that they haven't spoken with each other for so long" Matt said. The elevator stopped at the top floor which was the fifth floor, its doors opened up and James and Matt stepped out along with a group of female JBI agents. The women headed left down a hallway,

James and Matt was met at the elevator by Kimberly Anrhime "hi I tried to get in contact with Hayden but no reply, I just got off the phone with the mayor" she told James and Matt "what did he say" Matt asked her "he wants answers on what's being done to catch this person" Kimberly replied "great, that's all we need is the mayor coming down on us" James said. "I think Lorne has something to show you" she told James and Matt, Kimberly walked with them to Lorne's office "can you let Hayden know that the mayor is going to be here tomorrow" she asked James and Matt "I'll let him know" James said "he must be in a area with bad reception" Kimberly said. They were just outside Lorne's office, Kimberly left them and went to her office, James opened the door to the office and they both went in "hey how you guys doing" Lorne asked them without shifting his eyes off his computer screen "not too bad" James replied and continued "I heard you have something for us" he said to Lorne. "Yes I do, at the Julie Castorac crime scene, Crime Scene Investigators found a gum-wrapper on the marina's boardwalk near the bushes where she was found, they powdered the wrapper for finger prints and found one so they did a I.D match and discovered it belongs to a Terry Norman Willis, at the time he was twenty-four years old working in maintenance at North Brookshore General Hospital, the authorities didn't question him too hard because he lived in the area" Lorne informed them "that's why they should of questioned him" Matt said abruptly "well they figured it probably fell out of his pocket or he tossed it when he was on a walk" Lorne added "did you inform Hayden about this" James asked Lorne "I left a message on his phone" Lorne replied. "You want to go for a ride up to North Brookshore Hospital" James turned and asked Matt "I'm game" Matt replied as he checked some unrelated messages on his phone "I'll call Hayden on my way up there" James told Lorne "okay sounds good" Lorne replied and continued "remember take the PBP straight up, it will lead you there" Lorne told them. "Don't worry I know a quicker route" James assured him "which is" Lorne asked intrigued "take Silvercreek Road west to Magenta Tree Lane and that takes you right in front of the hospital" James replied and headed out the door followed by Matt.

(Embedded Narrative)
MORRIS ON HIS
FIFTIETH BIRTHDAY

The time of day was just about dusk, in a double-size trailer on the south end of Tilliquimsara Beach lives Morris Elgin a nature and animal photographer for Earth Daily Magazine right here in Brookshore. Morris was in the living room of his trailer sitting on a brown-leather couch eating dinner and watching TV, after work he had stopped off at the Barbecue Hut on Magenta Tree Lane and Mellongrove Avenue, he ordered Sambar deer ribs and potato wedges. He was now at home enjoying his dinner and watching the TV show 'Into The Night', that was one of his favorite show, that and '9-1-1: Lone Star'. Morris tossed the bare rib bones into a small garbage can that was next to the couch. Morris was an individual in every sense of the word, he was never married, doesn't have any kids, back when Morris was in his teens and twenties he never had a steady girlfriend. There's a secret that Morris has been keeping to himself ever since he was a teenager, something that he's not ashamed about but knows if he told other people they would look at him as some kind of freak. Morris finished eating his dinner and brought the empty plate to the kitchen, after he finishes watching his show he's going to look at some photos he took in Beryl Rado. He started washing the plate in the sink, as he washed his plate he looked down at the birthday card his mother sent him, she sent it to his workplace because she knew most of the time he was at work behind his desk. Morris stared at the card, it reminded him that he was fifty years old, the sentiment on the card was a invitation to his parents place. Morris was originally from Amaryllis Jaiz, his parents moved to Brookshore when he was fourteen, they recently moved back to Amaryllis Jaiz about a year and a half ago. Morris could remember all the great backyard socials his parents hosted back when he was a kid, they made the best barbecue in the neighborhood, so he figured it wouldn't hurt to pay them a visit on his birthday. He thought 'from here to Amaryllis Jaiz, how much is that by cab', Morris looked up the distance in Google Maps on his phone "well that looks like about eighty dollars" he said to himself. Morris put his phone inside the inside pocket of the sports jacket he was wearing "I'll do it for mom and dad" he said to himself with a chuckle. Morris called a cab, before bringing him to Amaryllis Jaiz he would get it to bring him to the Polish Deli on Magenta Tree Lane and Palm Avenue. Palm Avenue is the most southern road you can drive on in Brookshore going east to west, from the east it turns into the Palm Avenue Bridge that goes over Hubber's Lake right into Amaryllis Jaiz, this was the route Morris planned to take with the cab. After Morris finished washing and drying his plate he was in the living room looking at the photos he took in Beryl Rado, most of them were of birds, the West Indian whistling duck, the Purple throated carib and the Loggerhead kingbird. These birds have recently migrated to Janoesha Harbour and were spotted near the Black Forest, so Earth Daily sent Morris out to Beryl Rado to take pictures of them, Morris had forty photos in total, the other photos were of plant-life that grew along the Sambar Horn River in the south central Black Forest region. Before looking at the photos Morris called a cab, Morris put away his photos in a black leather binder, he then went into his bedroom and grabbed a suitcase from underneath his bed and packed a change of clothes in it along with some toiletries. It didn't take the cab that long to get to his trailer, he heard it blowing its horn out front as he was getting dressed in the bedroom, Morris wore blue-jeans and a white t-shirt, over the t-shirt he wore a black leather three quarter length sports jacket and on his feet he wore sneakers. He grabbed the suitcase and headed outside, he locked the front door and headed down the porch-steps.

The light-blue cab drove up the gravel drive way and stopped in front of Morris's trailer, Morris was sitting on his front steps with the suitcase resting on the step between his legs. As the cab stopped and parked in front of him, he stood up and grabbed his suitcase, the cab-driver came out of the car and went around to open the trunk so Morris could put his suitcase in. "Thank you" Morris said to the driver as he rested his suitcase in the trunk, the cab-driver closed the trunk and went back into the cab, Morris opened the back door of the cab and went in closing the door behind him. "Where to sir" the driver asked him "we're going to Amaryllis Jaiz, 834 west Route 11" Morris replied, the driver typed the address into the cab's GPS system. The driver started up the cab and backed down the driveway, when he got onto the road he made a three point turn and headed west, the road they were driving on was a dirt-road until they were west of the PBP then it became a paved road named Coastal Point Avenue. The driver turned on the radio in the cab to a local station, 75.7 The Trogon broadcasting from south Amaryllis Jaiz, they play Soft-Rock music like Christopher Cross, America or Jerry Rafferty. Morris rolled down the window so he could feel the evening breeze on his face, he didn't mind visiting his parents, they were fun to be around the only thing was he was getting tired of his mom continuously asking him when is she going to eat cake, referring to when is he going to get married. Morris's main focus has never been women and a relationship but lately he feels like he's been consumed by loneliness and really does want some companionship, maybe he just thinks too far out of the box to get close to someone, Morris chuckled to himself at that thought. Morris could see through the window that the cab was now going south on Magenta Tree Lane, he assumed it would be making a right turn when it got to Palm Avenue. "You seem to know the area, are you from around here" Morris asked the driver "no Hannon, only been living in Brookshore three years" the driver replied "well you sure know your job" Morris complimented the driver. Morris could see Palm Avenue coming up, just then he heard a loud bang like a shot-gun blast, the cab started swerving and then veered off and stopped on the gravel should of the road. The driver turned around in his seat and looked at Morris "are you alright sir" he asked Morris "yeah, what was that" Morris replied "I believe we have a flat" the driver said as he opened the door and got out to check, the driver walked towards the back of the car and saw that one of the rear tires had been punctured he then looked on the road for what could have caused the flat and saw the neck of a broken whiskey bottle in the middle of the road. The driver went over to where the piece of glass was, picked it up and chucked it in the bushes nearby, he headed back to his cab, as he did so he looked around for any gas stations, he spotted one on the southeast corner of Magenta Tree Lane & Palm Avenue, Pit-Stop Gas Station its sign read. It was right next to Sapphire Nights, Games & Adult Lounge, the driver got back in his cab and slowly made his way over to the gas station, lucky for them there was hardly any traffic on the road this time of day. The gas station was right at the corner of the intersection on a graveled area with a parking lot in front of the convenience store that was attached onto the gas station and a garage. The driver parked the cab beside one of the gas-pumps "sir give me five minutes, I'm going to see if I can get a new tire" he told Morris "hold on a sec, am I going to have to pay for this extra time" Morris asked him concerned about the cab's meter "don't worry sir I'll subtract it off what you owe me" the driver replied "thank you" Morris said to him. The driver left the cab and headed for the front desk of the gas station, behind the front desk a young man was sitting wearing the Pit-Stop company shirt with blue khaki pants, he had long black wavy hair that he wore in a pony-tail, he looked to be in his early twenties or late teens maybe in college, that's what it looked like when the cab-driver came up to the front desk and he was sitting behind it reading a physics book. "Hi" the cab-driver said to him and looked at the young man's name tag pinned on the breast pocket of his shirt and continued "hi David my car got a flat and I was hoping to buy a tire off you and have it installed" he said to David "sure I can do that for you but the installation is going to take forty minutes to an hour" David informed him "that's fine" the cab-driver replied "just pull your car up in front of the garage" David told him, the cab-driver headed back to his car. Morris was sitting in the cab with the window still open looking over at the Sapphire Nights Adult Lounge, he heard about that place and the bad element that drinks there, the police are usually in there twice a week do to stabbings or customers getting too aggressive with the staff, it was a place Morris rather not be around, the armpit of Brookshore it was to him but he never been in there and he was up for trying anything once 'maybe I'll check it out on my way home from mom and dad's' Morris thought to himself. The driver came back to the cab, he sat behind the wheel with the driver's side door open "so it's going to take about an hour to get a new tire and install it" the driver informed Morris, Morris looked at the driver and then back over at Sapphire Nights "okay" he said to the driver. Morris was planning on buying a bottle of water and using the facilities at Sapphire Nights Adult Lounge, he got out of the cab's backseat and closed the door behind him "where are you going" the cab-driver asked him "I'll be back in a few minutes" Morris told him as he walked away without looking back "okay I'll be over at the garage" the cab-driver informed him "okay" Morris said in a soft voice still walking towards Sapphire Nights.

Parked on the gravel parking lot out front of Sapphire Nights was two Harley Davidson motorbikes, one was a light-blue 1951 pan-back and the other was a 1983 sportster. They belonged to the owners of Sapphire Nights, their bikes where the only things parked next to the Lounge, all the other cars and bikes were parked in public-parking behind the gas station. Inside Sapphire Nights looked sort of like a casino, its floor was covered with a checkered pattern carpet that was colored in different shades of purple, there was rows and rows of slot-machines. Down the aisles of slot-machines strippers walk in string-bikinis and lingerie asking customers for lap-dances, towards the back of the lounge there are a group of pool-tables and to the left of that is a bar, next to the bar is the girls and guys washrooms. It was fairly busy inside Sapphire Nights, the bar was packed with people watching the Kelo-ball playoffs on the flat-screen TV they had behind the bar. Lisa Namamak a twenty year old runaway turned stripper was in the girls washroom snorting cocaine off the back of a toilet in one of the stalls, she had been cot before doing it by one of the bouncers, this time if she's cot she will be fired. After snorting a few lines up her nose she wiped the remnants of cocaine off her nose onto the back of her hand and then wiped the back of her hand onto the leg of the skin-tight black yoga-pants she was wearing. Lisa got up from sitting on the toilet and left the stall, she went to one of the sinks in the washroom and looked at her face in the mirror, just then the club's manager barged in on her "WHAT THE HELL!" she screamed at him "this is the ladies washroom" she told him "what are you doing in here" he asked her "that's none of your business" she replied "where's the cocaine" the manager inquired "I don't know what you're talking about" she replied without looking at him, just continued to look in the mirror while putting on lipstick. The manager grabbed her purse that was hanging over her shoulder (causing her to mess up her lipstick) and looked in it, he found two small metal canisters, one was empty and the other was half filled with cocaine. The manager took the half filled canister and grabbed Lisa by the arm "hey let me go" she told him as she wiped the ruined lipstick off her mouth and face with a tissue, he escorted her out of the washroom and to the front door of Sapphire Nights "that was your last chance, you no longer have a job here" he told her as he brought her to the front door "but I need this job" she said to him "you should of thought about that when you decided on taking drugs in here" he told her. When the manager got to the front door with her he escorted her outside on the front porch of Sapphire Nights and gave her a slap on the butt "OW!" she screamed "don't come back without calling first" he told her and then went back inside. Lisa stood outside rubbing the sting out of her bottom "bastard" she said under her breath to the manager as he went back inside, not knowing what to do know 'without a job she can't stay at the motel she lives at and going home to two abusive parents was not an option for her' she thought to herself. She stood there now smoking a cigarette trying to figure out what to do.

As Morris came up to the front steps of Sapphire Nights he stared up at its large neon-blue sign, as he made his way up the steps he heard someone sobbing to the left of him. He turned and looked to see who it was, leaning up in a dark corner of the porch was a young girl, to Morris she didn't look any older than eighteen, she was crying and wiping her nose with a tissue she got out of her purse. She was wearing a purple cotton blouse with a low neckline that showed off her cleavich and black yoga pants that looked like they were painted on her athletic looking legs and round buttock, on her feet she wore a pair of white Converse sneakers. "Are you okay" Morris asked her, Lisa didn't notice that there was anyone on the porch until she heard a man's voice, she raised her head from her sorrowful worries to see a middle aged man looking at her "yeah everything is cool, no worries" she replied as she sniffled "it certainly doesn't look like it, it looks like someone shot your dog" Morris said to her "aw it's nothing you wouldn't understand" Lisa told him. Morris smiled at her "why because I'm old" he asked her and continued "maybe you should give me a chance to understand, I'm going in here to use their facilities, I'll be back out, if you're here you can tell me all about it" he told her "why do you care" Lisa asked him "I see a girl that can be my daughter crying in the corner of a place like this, it does concern me" Morris replied "I won't be long" he told her as he opened the door to Sapphire Nights and went in. Inside Sapphire Nights a live band was play on the stage that was setup to the right of a group of pool-tables, the band's name was Charlie & The Young Sporadics, they played a lot of Rhythm & Blues plus

Soft Rock, they were a local band from the area. Morris walked down a aisle of slot-machines to a bar he saw in the back, he was going to buy a bottle of water, on his way there he spotted a bouncer standing by one of the slot-machines "hi can you tell me where the washroom is" Morris asked as he walked up to the bouncer "yeah they're to your left just before you get to the bar" the bouncer replied as he pointed Morris in the direction of the washroom "thanks" Morris said and headed to the bar. As he got to the bar he seen the guys and gals washrooms to the left of the bar down a short hallway. Morris pulled up one of the wooden stools that were in front of the bar and sat down, the bartender at the other end of the bar spotted him and came over to see what he wanted "hey there welcome to Sapphire Nights what can I get for you" the bartender asked Morris as he came and wiped down the bar in front of him "a bottle of water please" Morris replied "sure thing" the bartender said and went to get the bottle of water. Morris sat there on the stool looking around the night-club as he waited for the bartender to bring him a bottle of water 'it's quite steady in here' Morris thought to himself 'not too busy but busy enough to keep the place going'. Morris began eating some pretzel-sticks on the bar in front him out of a glass-cup that had Sapphire Nights name on it, the bartender returned with Morris's water, he placed it on a coaster in front of Morris "a Bronze-piece please" (which is twenty-five cents in Janoesian money) the bartender said, Morris gave him a Silver-piece (which is fifty cents in Janoesian money) and took the bottle of water, he got off the stool and headed for the washroom. Morris went into the washroom and used one of the urinals after that he went over to the sink to wash his hands. As he turned on the tap and soaked his hands under the lukewarm water and started inspecting himself in the mirror, looking at how much grey hair he had in his beard and mustache "I must look really old to her" he said to himself as he looked for any wrinkles on his face. Morris was pleased to know that a lot of people at work couldn't believe he was turning fifty, they thought he was in his early to mid forties "well you can't turn back the clock" he said to himself as he continued to look at himself in the mirror. Morris turned off the tap and dried his hands with a bunch of brown paper towels he got out of the paper-towel dispenser mounted on the wall beside him. After he chucked the wad of wet paper towels in the garbage-can by the sink he took his bottle of water off the sink and left the washroom. Morris came out of the washroom's hallway back into the night-club, the band Charlie & The Young Sporadics were doing a cover of a Led Zeppelin song (Over The Hills And Far Away), Morris opened the bottle of water and started drinking as he made his way to the front door of Sapphire Nights. When Morris came back outside he saw Lisa sitting on the steps smoking a cigarette "still here I see" Morris said to her as he let the door close behind him "I don't know where to go" she said to him "what brought you here" Morris asked her "I used to work here" she replied "great! maybe you can get someone inside to drive you to where you need to be" Morris told her "it's a little more complicated than that, look you don't need to be wasting anymore time with someone like me, I can handle myself" Lisa told him as she flicked away the cigarette butt and stood up to get out of Morris's way. Morris came down the steps to where Lisa was standing "are you hungry, can I at lease get you something to eat" he asked her, she was concerned about his generous hospitality 'either he's up to something or he's some kind of social worker' she thought to herself "are you a cop" she asked him "no I'm a photographer" Morris replied. She looked him up and down, he looked like a normal head-strong man that works 9 to 5 to her "where do you work" she inquired "Earth Daily here in Brookshore" Morris replied, Morris could see that she was concern for her safety so he reached into the breast pocket of his sport jacket and took out a business-card, he gave it to her. Lisa looked at the card and then back at Morris "okay just for something to eat and no funny business" she told him "promise, it's only to get you something to eat" he assured her "by the way my name is Morris" he told her as he extended his hand "Lisa" she replied and they shook hands. Morris escorted Lisa to the taxi-cab that was parked in the garage next to the gas station "so you didn't answer my question back there" Morris said to her as they walked to the garage "which was" Lisa asked him "what brings you out here" Morris asked Lisa still wondering why she would be in a place like Sapphire Nights "I told you I use to work there" she replied wondering why he would ask her that again. Morris knew there was more to Lisa's reply but wasn't sure what it was "well that's no place for someone like you to be working" he told her, Lisa smiled at Morris's comment. When they got to the garage Morris could see that the cab was on a jack and a mechanic was putting on a new tire "should only take a few more minutes" Morris told Lisa "we can wait out here" he informed her. So they stood out in front of the gas station's convenience store waiting for the cab's wheel to be changed "do you mind if I smoke" Lisa asked Morris "no go ahead" he replied. Lisa took a pack of cigarettes out of her purse "would you like one" she offered Morris as she took one out of the pack "no thank you" he replied and then gave her a subtle smile, Lisa saw in Morris's face youthfulness even though he had a salt and pepper beard, he looked to be in good health to her. She lit the cigarette with a Zippo-lighter she had in her purse and inhaled her lungs full of smoke and then exhaled, a cloud of smoke came out her nostrils and mouth "so are you married" she asked Morris "no not married" Morris replied as he played solitaire on his cell-phone "were you ever married" Lisa inquired "no never married" Morris replied "so never been married, any kids" she asked him "no kids" Morris replied as he continued to play solitaire on his phone. Morris stopped playing with his phone and looked around to see how much progress the gas station's mechanic had made in changing the tire "hmm" he said to himself "not too long now" he told Lisa, Lisa looked over at the mechanic in the garage then back at Morris, she was wondering how come a man his age doesn't have any kids "how come you never got married" she asked him "just wasn't in the cards" Morris replied. Morris didn't feel comfortable talking about stuff like that "do you want something to drink" he asked Lisa, doing his best to change the subject "yeah a six of Blue Toucan" she replied jokingly "lets stick to the non-alcoholic beverages" Morris told her "boy! you're boring" Lisa said as she rolled her eyes at Morris and continued "okay a can of Coke" she told him "a can of Coke coming right up" Morris said to her as he left her there and went in the store "Cherry-Coke if they have it" she told him before the front door to the store closed. Lisa didn't know what she was going to do after she got something to eat but at lease at the present time she was in good company, maybe later she'll get him to drop her off at one of the InnerHoop stations 'we'll see how it goes' she thought to herself. Morris came back out holding two cans of Coke, one was a Cherry-Coke, he gave the Cherry-Coke to Lisa "thank you" she said "you're welcome" Morris replied. Lisa opened her coke and started drinking "where are you headed to" Lisa asked Morris "Amaryllis Jaiz to my parents place" Morris replied "what for" Lisa inquired "to spend my birthday with them" Morris told her "it's your birthday, happy birthday" she said to him "thank you" Morris replied "how old are you today" Lisa asked him "how old do I look" Morris replied "early forties, forty-one forty-two maybe" she said "I'm fifty" Morris replied. The cab driver came out of the garage and went over to where Morris and Lisa were standing "okay the car should be ready in the next ten minutes" he informed Morris "okay sounds good, by the way we have a new passenger" Morris told the cab driver "not a problem sir" the cab driver replied and headed back to the garage. Morris looked at Lisa "have you ever been to Amaryllis Jaiz" he asked her "I guess, when I was a kid" she replied, Morris smiled at her reply, to him she was still a kid "well there's a great restaurant their called Burks Den you'll enjoy it" he told her. "I remember seeing a lot of flowers when I was there" Lisa told Morris "yes it's the City Of Flowers" Morris said. The mechanic in the garage released the hydraulic pressure from the jack under the cab and the cab came slowly down to the ground as the jack hid its self in the ground underneath the cab "okay it's all done sir" the mechanic told the cab driver "thank you" the cab driver replied as he got into the driver's seat of the cab. He started up the car and drove it out of the garage and over to where Morris and Lisa were standing "oh look our ride is here" Morris said to Lisa, the cab stopped in front of them, Morris opened the back door so Lisa could get in, as soon as she got in and sat down Morris followed behind her and shut the door. The cab left the gas station, turned left onto Palm Avenue and headed west to the Palm Avenue Bridge.

It was now nighttime on Janoesha Harbour the sun had gone completely down, the cab sped along the Palm Avenue Bridge, the cab-driver was doing his best not to go over the speed limit. Morris felt at ease in the back seat with his new best friend, Lisa had the window open, she was taking in the scenery along the bridge and she also liked the warm breeze blowing through her hair. She stared out at the lights that were mounted on the guard-rail of the bridge, she also saw the city lights of Amaryllis Jaiz in the distance reflecting off Hubber's Lake creating ghostly streaks of bright majestic colors. "Lovely view isn't it" Morris said to her as he noticed her gazing through the window "yeah it's beautiful" Lisa replied. Just then the cab-driver saw a white van parked on the shoulder of the bridge, it's back doors were open. It was on the other side of the road so the cab-driver kept slowly driving by to see if there was anyone in need of help. After the cab passed by the van Morris and Lisa could see through the back window a young man holding something wrapped in a white red stained bed-sheet and bound with duct tape, there were weights also taped to the bed-sheet, he tossed it over the bridge, it made a loud splash when it hit the water below. The young man turned around to see a cab and Morris and Lisa staring at him from it's back window. Morris realized that he saw them and told the cab-driver to drive faster. The young man went around the back of the van and closed it's doors as he went inside. He then went up front and sat in the driver's seat, at this time the cab was out of his site. He started up the van and headed in the same direction as the cab.

The young man driving the white van is thirty-three year old Joe Shilo, a month ago he was released from jail after doing a five year stretch for domestic abuse. He had beaten his wife severely, putting her in the hospital, his wife is thirty year old Imogene Shilo. Ten days ago she asked him to sign some divorce papers, they met at her lawyer's office, Joe refused to sign the papers and told her lawyer that whatever problems him and his wife is going through they can work it out on there own and they don't need any help from no one. Imogene had moved away with their five year old daughter into her own place, in fear of Joe Imogene filed a restraining order against him. She had moved to the other side of the city to get away from him, six days ago she was reported missing by one of her co-workers at the restaurant she works at. As he drove Joe looked around to see if he could spot the cab, he needed to find the cab, they had saw something that they shouldn't have.

As the Palm Avenue Bridge enters Amaryllis Jaiz it turns into Route 9, the cab was now driving on Route 9 through the upper-middle class neighborhood of Cobbled Palm. "Was that a dead body he threw in the water" Lisa asked Morris referring to what they just saw back on the bridge "it sure looked like it" Morris replied. "We need to call the cops" Lisa told him concerned for her safety "we will, as soon as we get to Burks Den" Morris replied. "Where do you want to go sir, the police station or the restaurant" the cab-driver asked Morris, Morris thought about it for a second "the restaurant" he replied "okay" the cab-driver complied as he turned on the radio. A song by Christopher Cross had just finish playing and the news came on, on the news it stated that the police was looking for thirty year old Imogene Faye Shilo she was reported missing six days ago. The authorities also wanted to speak with her husband Joesph Dean Shilo but he's nowhere to be found, the police say he owns a white Dodge van, him and his van is now the middle of a police investigation. "Can you turn that up please" Morris asked the cab-driver, the cab-driver turned the radio up. Morris listened carefully to the news "I wonder if that's the white van we saw on the bridge" Lisa asked Morris "I'm not too sure" Morris replied as he continued to listen to the news "who else could it be" Lisa said concerned for her safety. Lisa fished around in her purse for her cell-phone "I'm calling the cops" she told Morris as she took her cell-phone out of her purse. Morris put his hand on her hand she had holding the phone preventing her from making the call "you don't want to do that just yet, lets be sure that's the right van before we call the cops" he told her, she agreed and put the phone back in her purse. The news had finished and the cab-driver turned down the volume on the radio, the cab turned into the parking lot of Burks Den, the driver found an empty parking spot near the front door. "How are you going to find out if that's the right van" Lisa asked Morris "I'll figure something out" Morris replied, he opened the door and got out of the cab, being the gentleman that he was he left the door open so Lisa could get out. "Sir I'll wait here, take your time I turned off the meter" the cab-driver told Morris "thank you" Morris said to the cab-driver, him and Lisa went into Burks Den. They sat down at a table that was beside a large window so they could see who came into the parking lot. There was a clear jug of water on the table with two glass cups, Lisa picked up the jug and poured herself a glass of water "so what would you like to eat" Morris asked her "can we wait a little, I'm still a little shaking up from what I just saw" she said "sure not a problem" Morris replied. Morris looked at Lisa as she poured herself another glass of water "can I ask you a question, please don't take offense" he asked her "okay I guess" she replied "were you working as a stripper back there" he asked her referring to Sapphire Nights. She looked at him with a blank expression on her face "would you think less of me if I was" she asked him "no of course not, it's a job like any other" Morris replied, "but I think you can do much better" he added "oh yeah, really, like what" she asked him. Morris looked at her like a dad concerned about his child's welfare "you look to be in your early twenties or younger, how bout taking a course in college" he asked her "sitting behind a desk doesn't really interest me" she replied. A waitress came to their table, she put down two menus on the table "can I get you anything to drink" the waitress asked as she stood there with a pen and note pad "yes a Blue Toucan for me and a Mountain Dew for the young lady" Morris replied "coming right up" the waitress said "oh and can you bring a straw also" Morris added before the waitress left "sure thing sir" the waitress said and then left. Morris looked at Lisa sitting across from him "so where do you live" he asked her "are you asking where I'm from or where I live now" Lisa asked him "no need to get defensive, I'm not going to attack or hurt you" Morris said in a soft voice. "Well if you really need to know I'm from south Umni" Lisa said finally giving into Morris's subtle manner "where do you live now" Morris asked her "I have a room at the Draydon Motel" Lisa replied "I know that place, that's no place for someone like you to be" he told her. She felt ashamed telling him this, like her life wasn't worth nothing, but Morris made her feel like a person, like she belonged "it's just until I get back on my feet" she informed him. She looked outside through the window, looking to see if she could spot the white van coming in the parking lot, Morris also took a glance outside "calm down we're going to be okay" he assured Lisa as he put his hand on her shoulder "I think maybe I need to freshen up in the washroom a little" she told him "yeah sure there's a hallway to the right of the salad bar, straight down there are the washrooms" he directed her with his hand. Lisa got up and headed to the washroom. Morris sat there looking outside, soon after the waitress showed up with their drinks "a Mountain Dew for the lady and a Blue Toucan for you sir" the waitress placed their drinks on the table "thank you" Morris said to her. Morris could see Lisa in the distance coming from the washroom holding a clump of tissue in her hand. Morris turned and looked out the window again, he saw a white van pull into the restaurant's parking lot and park three spots away from the taxi-cab. Morris immediately ducked down under the table "GET DOWN" he signaled with his hand for Lisa to do. Lisa hid behind the salad-bar "GO TO THE WASHROOM AND STAY THERE UNTIL I SAY" Morris told her, so she quickly made her way back into the washroom. Morris peeked up over the table and through the window and saw a young man get out the driver's side of the van and head over to where his taxi-cab was. The man started talking with the cab-driver, suddenly he pulled a gun out of his pants and pointed it at the cab-driver, Morris heard a loud popping sound like a fire-cracker going off, the cab-driver's head slumped over the cab's door and out its open window as blood dripped from his temple onto the ground. This is when Morris realized his cab-driver just got shot, Morris did his best walking on his hands and knees, he was heading for the mop room, he would hide in there just in case this guy comes in here. On the way to the mop room he knocked on the ladies washroom to warn Lisa "STAY IN THERE DON'T COME OUT" he told her. Morris hid in the mop room across from the washrooms. The restaurant was fairly empty at this time of the night, only a couple people sitting at the bar. From the mop room Morris could hear the restaurant's front door swing open and the bells over top of it jingling. A young man walked into Burks Den, his right arm that was holding a 45 Colt Revolver was splattered with blood, specks of blood were also dappled on his t-shirt. All the employees in Burks Den stopped what they were doing and stared at the young man, the man walked up to the bar "hey I'm looking for a man and a woman that came in here recently" he asked the bartender, the bartender was very nervous he didn't know what to say, he was worried about the gun the man was holding and the fact that he was covered in blood "sorry I didn't see anyone" the bartender replied. The restaurant manager came out of his office that was behind the bar, he walked up to the man standing in front of the bar "hi I'm John the manager, how can I help you" John asked the man "I'm looking for two people a man and a woman" the man replied. John looked at the man's bloodied arm and went to offer him aid "you look hurt, can I call you an ambulance" John asked him, the man raised up his arm and fired a shot into the ceiling "YOU'RE NOT LISTENING!" the man screamed, the gun shot made everyone gasp in fear. "Okay calm down, I don't believe they came in here" John said to him, the young man pointed at the taxi-cab outside "they were in that cab not too long ago" he told John as John turned his head back to face him from looking at the cab outside "I guess they must of gotten dropped off before it got here" John said. "I guess I could believe that but I don't trust you John" the man said to John as he pointed his gun at him "so I'm going to take a look around just to make sure, is that cool with you John" he added as he cocked the hammer back on his gun and smiled at John "sure feel free to look around" John instinctively replied "good answer" the man said and slowly released the hammer. The man got all the employees and whatever customers were in the restaurant to come out to the middle of the restaurant. "Okay you're with me" the man said as he grabbed a young waitress by the hair, pulling her violently close to him "you John collect everybody's phone and whatever computer devices they have on them and put them in this bag" the man gave John a plastic-bag, John went around collecting everyone's phone. Just then a special bulletin came over a small TV that was mounted on the wall over the bar, it stated that the police was looking for a Joe Shilo in the disappearance of his wife Imogene Shilo. The TV showed a picture of Joe Shilo beside it was reward money ($15,000) from Imogene's parents in any information that leads to the capture and conviction of Joe Shilo. Joe looked at himself on TV "they could have used a better picture" he said and fired a shot through the screen of the TV, the TV imploded as white-smoke billowed out of its distorted cracks. People gasped and shrieked in fear to the sound of gun fire. John finished collecting everyone's phone "okay put the bag over there" Joe pointed to the hallway next to the salad bar, so John did as he was told. "Okay me and this young lady are going to check the washrooms, if anyone tries anything I'll put a bullet in her head" Joe told the group of people as he backed up with the waitress, holding her around the shoulders close to him "lets go" he whispered to her. They headed for the washrooms "ladies first" Joe told the waitress, Joe held the waitress in front of him so she would be the one to open the door.

As Morris hid in the mop room he could hear movement just outside the door, he also heard a lady sniffling and crying begging someone not to kill her "calm down and open it" an unknown male voice said. To Morris it sound like they were right across the hall 'that could only mean they were about to enter into the ladies washroom' he thought to himself. Morris couldn't let this happen, Lisa was in there, Morris looked down at a metal mop-ringer sitting in a yellow-plastic bucket. He opened the door a crack to see where they were, they were about to enter into the ladies washroom, he grabbed the handle of the ringer and lifted it out of the bucket, with his other hand he slowly opened up the door, moving ever so stealthily he crepted up behind Joe and struck him over the back of the head with the mop-ringer. Joe went down like a tree in the forest with a severed trunk, as his body hit the polished hardwood in the hallway the gun slid out of his hand, Morris picked it up and put it in his jacket pocket, he opened the washroom door to let Lisa out. Lisa looked at Joe laying on the floor as she came out of the washroom "oh my God, is he dead" she asked Morris "no just out cold for now" Morris replied. John came over to where Joe was laying after hearing all the commotion "are you okay" he asked Morris and Lisa "yeah we're fine" Morris replied "do you have any rope so I can tie this guy up" Morris asked John "yes we got some in the back" John replied. John took the waitress back to where everyone was sitting in the restaurant, he sat her down and the bartender got her a glass of water while John went to get some rope for Morris. "We should check if the cab-driver is alright" Lisa said to Morris "he's not I seen him get shot by this guy" Morris told her "oh no is he dead" she asked him "yeah I'm pretty sure he is" Morris replied. John came back with some rope, Morris and John sat Joe in one of the chairs in the restaurant and put him in front of the bar, they had lots of rope to use, they tied Joe up to the chair he was sitting in with his hands tied behind his back, he was still out cold. "Okay sir what's your name" Morris asked John "John Moawabae I'm the manager here" John replied "John call the police and tell them there has been a shooting and a murder here" Morris told John. John headed to his office to use the phone while Morris and Lisa stayed and watched over Joe, they sat down around a table next to where Joe was "so what do we do now" Lisa asked Morris "now we wait for the police, it's called a citizen's arrest" he replied "okay" she said "and also we give them this" Morris took the gun out of his jacket pocket and rest it on the table. "Hey how come you have that" Lisa asked Morris surprise to see him with a gun "it fell out of his hand when he went down, and I picked it up" Morris replied "your fingerprints are on that now" she told him "no need to worry I have all these witnesses on my side plus there's security-cameras in here and outside" he informed Lisa. John came to the table they were sitting at "okay the police are on their way right now" John informed Morris and Lisa "thank you John" Morris said, John went back to where the rest of the employees and customers were. Morris and Lisa sat around the table and waited till the police came "you're right, it is a nice place" Lisa said looking around the restaurant "too bad I couldn't romance you with a candle-light dinner" Morris replied jokingly, Lisa gave him a warm smile "so I guess meeting your parents is on delay" Lisa asked him, Morris didn't exactly know what she meant by that "I'm not too sure what you mean by that" Morris said "weren't you on your way to see them" Lisa asked him "yeah that's true, but I don't mind the delay at lease I found a friend" he replied as he smiled at her. Lisa giggled and smiled at Morris's compliment "well I hope you're enjoying your birthday, minus the part when you met up with that guy" Lisa said to Morris as she pointed at Joe still out cold in the chair "it couldn't be better" Morris replied. At this time they could here the police sirens coming in the distance, Morris put the gun back in his pocket and stood up from around the table, Lisa stood up with him and put both her hands around his arm "my hero, maybe later we could solve some of your social problems" she hinted to him as she held him close. Morris smiled as he left the restaurant with Lisa to meet the police out front, at this time Joe was just waking up.

THROUGH TERRY'S EYES

Hayden and Ravi were parked at a burger joint not too far from Madam Zebandee's place, they were taking a bit of a break before heading back to Brookshore. Ravi was in the limo eating a cheese burger and Hayden was sitting around one of the few picnic tables that's out in front of the burger joint, he was drinking a strawberry shake and about to call Lorne. Hayden heard the phone ring, Lorne picked up on the second ring "All-Capable-Lorne at your service" Lorne answered "hey Lorne it's Hayden I'm going to send you the name, model and license plate number of a car, I need you to find the owner's name" Hayden informed him "okay will do" Lorne replied "I just sent it to your email" Hayden told him "okay I'll have it for you in ten minutes" Lorne said. Hayden also listened to the message Lorne left on his voice-mail 'Terry Norman Willis, the name doesn't ring a bell' Hayden thought "too bad he didn't send a picture" he said to himself. Hayden finished his shake and tossed the empty cup in a garbage-can nearby, he got up from around the table and went back to the limo. "Hey how you doing with that burger" Hayden asked Ravi as he opened the door and sat in the back seat "I finished it, working on the fries now" Ravi replied. Hayden had a laptop in a bag on the seat beside him, he took it out of the bag and rested it on his lap, he opened the screen by unlocking it with a password. He was doing a name-search for the name Terry Norman Willis through the JBI's website 'maybe I'll find out what vehicle he drives' Hayden thought "I wonder if T stands for Terry" Hayden said to himself. Ravi over-heard him and thought he was addressing him "I'm not too sure sir, maybe" Ravi replied "pardon me" Hayden said as he raised his eyes up from the computer-screen. Ravi turned in his seat to face Hayden, now realizing that Hayden was on his laptop deep in thought "sorry sir I thought you were asking me a question" he said. "That's alright" Hayden said as he stared at his computer screen, on the screen a profile for Terry Norman Willis came up, the profile was from 1994 when Terry got arrested for shoplifting, it showed a young Terry Willis at twenty-five years old. It also showed the vehicle that he owned, it was a 1989 Plymouth Reliant, smoke-grey in color 'wrong vehicle' he thought to himself "maybe he changed vehicles by then" Hayden whispered to himself. Ravi had just finished off his fries and put the empty paper-bag on the seat beside him, he put his drink in the limo's center consul "where to sir" he asked Hayden "lets head back to the office" Hayden replied. Ravi started up the limo and backed out of the burger joint's parking lot onto Route 9 and headed east.

James and Matt just pulled up into the outdoor lobby of North Brookshore General Hospital, James parked out front, they got out of the SUV and headed into the hospital "where's the best place to check first" Matt asked "I would say human resources" James replied. Inside the hospital's lobby injured and ill people sat waiting to see a doctor, its hallways were lined with empty and occupied gurneys, and busy with nurses and nurse-aids pushing patients in wheel-chairs. James and Matt headed down the hallway that had a sign that read Human Resources, the sign directed them downstairs to the basement, when they got down to the basement they turned right from the staircase they were on and the human resources office was the second door down the hall on the right. Matt opened the door to the human resources office and allowed James to go in first "after you sir" Matt said jokingly as he entered into the office behind James. James walked up to the customer service desk "hi Special Agent James Morris for the JBI" he said as he showed his badge to the young lady sitting behind the customer service desk "who's in charge of the archives down here" he asked the lady, she reluctantly looked at Matt standing beside James "don't worry he's with me" he assured the young lady, Matt showed her his badge. The lady looked back at James "what name are you looking for officer" she asked James "Terry Willis" James replied "okay give me a few minutes" she told James and then got up from behind her desk and went in the back. Matt didn't understand what was going on "why couldn't she just let us back there to look for ourselves" Matt asked James "everything is confidential here, they don't want no one looking at anyone's file" James replied "how do the courts get around that" Matt inquired "the courts are the only ones that can lift the confidentiality" James replied. The young lady came back to her desk holding a thick paper file in a folder and a floppy-disk "here we go" she said as she rest the file on her desk "this is for you" she added as she gave the floppy-disk to James, Matt turned the folder around on the desk so it was right side up, he flipped through its pages.

"You know I wasn't here when Terry worked here but Rose was" the lady told James "where does Rose work" James asked her "she works in the back" the lady replied "may I speak with her" James asked her "sure I'll get her for you" she replied and went to the back. Not long after she came back out with Rose, Rose was a middle age lady, she had shoulder length hair that was died maroon-red "Rose these men are JBI agents they want to ask you about Terry Willis" she informed Rose. "Yeah I knew Terry back then" Rose said to James and Matt "what sort of person was he back then" Matt asked Rose "he was very quiet, kept to himself and always did what he was told" Rose replied, Matt looked down at the file "it says here that he was born May 12th,1969, that would have made him twenty-five years old at the time, did he have a girlfriend or a wife" Matt inquired "oh no Terry wasn't that kind of person he seemed very shy, plus he was very obedient to his father" Rose replied. "Where can we find his father" James asked Rose "at the cemetery, his dad died in 1996" Rose replied, Matt closed back the file and held it in his hand "can we take this, I promise that it will be returned to you" Matt asked Rose "what's this all about, is Terry okay" Rose asked not too sure of what was going on "everything is okay Miss" Matt replied "it's Mrs, Mrs. Teltin" Rose said abrupted. "Mam everything is okay where here to find out where Terry is, we just need to borrow this file for a few days I promise I'll bring it back" James said in a calm voice to Rose, assuring her that everything was okay "okay if you're going to return it that's fine" Rose said to James "thank you Mrs.Teltin" James said to her and shook her hand.

It was now 10:30pm in Brookshore and at RL Home Outfitters building, manager Dana Hollinger was finishing up some paperwork in her office, it had been a long day for her and she was looking forward to getting home and soaking her feet in the bathtub while drinking a glass of red wine. Dana initialed the last sheet of paper, after that she put away all the paperwork in her desk drawer, she grabbed her purse and headed out the door. Dana worked on the fifth floor, she was now in the elevator going down to the ground-floor. The elevator stopped at the ground-floor and its doors opened up, Dana stepped out into the front lobby, she waved bye to the security-guard that was on duty at the front desk as she left through the front door, he waved back.

Terry was parked a block away from RL Home Outfitters under a Avocado tree. He sat in his car with a pair of binoculars spying and watching to see when the red Pontiac Sunfire would leave out of the gated building. He didn't have to wait too long, the gate opened up and a red Pontiac Sunfire came out of the buildings entrance and turned left on Silvercreek Road, as soon as it did so Terry started up his Mustang and followed at a safe distance behind.

Dana had gotten a call from her roommate while she was driving, it was okay because she was wearing a Blue Tooth headset. Her roommate wanted her to pick up some milk and toilet paper because they were fresh out "okay I'll stop off at Marks 1 Variety, I'll see you when I get home" she told her roommate and then ended the call. Dana made a left turn on Kamper Avenue, Marks 1 Variety wasn't too far down from Silvercreek & Kamper Avenue. Dana picked this store because it was close to Glory Meadows Blvd where she lived, the store was only a couple blocks away from her actual place. She pulled into the store's parking lot, got out of the car and went into the store, inside Marks 1 Variety was respectively busy with customers, the store was fairly large like a small market. Dana really just wanted to get home, she was tired so she grabbed the things she needed and headed to the cashier's counter. After paying for her items she left the store and went back to her car, Dana put the bag of groceries on top of her car and went to get her car keys out of her purse when she was bull rushed, knocked out by a fist and carried away.

The next morning at 9:15am a missing person's call came into 661 Emergency by Dana's roommate, she told the operator that the last time she spoke with Dana she was heading to Marks 1 Variety on Kamper

Avenue. The police headed to Marks 1 Variety, when they got there they found an abandon Pontiac Sunfire with a bag of groceries on top of it. Not too long after Byron Phelps showed up "what happened here" he asked a officer on the scene "missing person it looks like sir" the officer replied. Before Byron could get out of his cruiser a call came through reporting that they found a body at Canna Striata Gardens in Amaryllis Jaiz, the identification on the victim stated that she lived in Brookshore. Byron called Hayden "hi Agent Alexander I need you to meet me at Canna Striata Gardens in Amaryllis Jaiz, I think I got something, a body was found out there" he left a message on Hayden's voice-mail. Byron called over one of the officers to his car "have someone run the license plate number on the car" he told the officer "we already did sir the owner is a Dana Hollinger she's thirty-five years old and lives here in Brookshore at 518 Glory Meadows Blvd, the same address as the 661 caller" the officer informed Byron. "Okay I'm heading to Amaryllis Jaiz, I won't be long, let everyone know to keep the search going and make sure you bring the car back to the lab to get super-glued for fingerprints" Byron told the young officer.

Hayden was at the JBI office doing some paperwork when Kimberly knocked on his open door "good morning Kim how are you" he asked her "a call just came in for you on the conference phone, they found a body in Amaryllis Jaiz at Canna Striata Gardens" she informed Hayden "I believe it was a Major Byron Phelps that called" she added "thank you Kim, can you have Lorne get me directions to Canna Striata Gardens" he said to her "not a problem sir" Kimberly replied and then left his office. Hayden grabbed his sports jacket from around the chair he was sitting in and his hat from off his desk and left his office. On the way to the elevator he ran into James and Matt "where are you heading to" James asked him "they found a body in Amaryllis Jaiz, I'm heading out there to meet up with Chief Phelps" Hayden replied as he put his jacket on and pressed the down button on the elevator. "So how did it go at the hospital" Hayden asked James "it went well, we got a file on Terry Willis and according to someone that knew him their Terry was a good guy that kept to himself" James replied "if he kept to himself how do they know that he was a good guy" Hayden said "do you think the body in Amaryllis Jaiz is connected to these murders" Matt ask Hayden "realistically I'm not sure but in my gut I believe so" Hayden replied. One of the three elevators opened and Hayden stepped in "meet me in Amaryllis Jaiz later" Hayden told James and Matt as the elevator's door closed.

When Hayden got to Canna Striata Gardens there was three police cruisers out front with a coroner's van. Hayden got out of the limo "I won't be long" he told Ravi and went into the gardens. Canna Striata Gardens is a free garden, anyone can go in and see the flowers, it's also an outdoor garden that's open 24/7, it's a very large garden that has wicker-chairs and fancy coffee-tables in its picnicking area. As Hayden came up to where the police were he could see a female body laying on a small area of neatly cut Augustine-grass surrounded by palm-bushes. Byron turned his head to see Hayden standing beside him "is this another one" he asked Hayden "well lets hope for the best" Hayden replied as he stooped down to get a better look at the body "who's in charge here" Hayden asked Byron while he studied the body "you are if it turns out that the body is connected to the ones in Brookshore" a man's voice replied, it didn't sound like Byron's voice to Hayden, he turned his head to see who it was, a large bald dark-skin black man was looking down at him. The man held out his hand to greet him "Oscar Rambuutae nice to meet you, I'm chief of police here in Amaryllis Jaiz" they shook hands. "Who found the body" Hayden asked Oscar "couple teenage lovers came here for a early morning quickie and stumbled upon her" Oscar replied "looks like a body-dump to me" Oscar added "she's only wearing a bra, did you find other items of clothes" Hayden asked Oscar "no just a purse in the bushes, the I.D in it says that she's Dana Hollinger from Brookshore" Oscar replied "did you say Dana Hollinger" Byron abruptly asked Oscar "yes Dana Hollinger" Oscar repeated "in Brookshore we received a 661 call from someone that reported a missing person, we went to the last place she was and found an abandon car with a bag of groceries on it, we ran the plates and it came back Dana Hollinger" Byron informed them. "It sounds like that's where he abducted her" Hayden said, he looked at her vaginal area and saw metal specks "yep it's our guy" Hayden said "why did he dump the body over city-lines" Oscar asked Hayden "to throw us off his track" Hayden replied. Hayden turned and looked up at Byron "I need to process her car" he told Byron "its been sent to our police-lab to be super-glued for fingerprints" Byron informed him "okay tell them not to touch the interior" Hayden told him "will do" Byron complied and left to go to his cruiser. Hayden wasn't too sure about the body been dumped in Amaryllis Jaiz 'does he have family here' Hayden thought "maybe" Hayden said to himself as he stood up (Hayden had a hunch) "can I get two of your cruisers to head over to Slaps Bed & Breakfast" Hayden said to Oscar "yeah I know the place, I'll have them head over right now" Oscar replied "tell them to ask the madam if a T has come in" Hayden told him "sure thing" Oscar complied. Oscar called for two units to head over to Slaps Bed & Breakfast, he also told them what to ask the madam "thank you" Hayden said to Oscar "not a problem, only thing is, is, what's the connection to Slaps" Oscar asked him "just a hunch I have" Hayden replied "well it's your case if you need any help let me know" Oscar told him "it's nice to know that thank you" Hayden replied, they shook hands as the coroner took the body. "I'll be following the coroner" Oscar told Hayden, Hayden gave him a card "call me later to let me know how to get there" Hayden told him, Oscar took the card and headed to his cruiser. Hayden was planning on heading to Slaps to see if the police there found something or if he could ID who the killer is. On the way back to the limo Hayden gave James a call "hi James it's Hayden I need you to go to Marks 1 Variety on Kamper Avenue near Silvercreek, take a picture of Terry Willis with you and see if the cashier there seen anyone that looked like him, I'll be at Slaps Bed & Breakfast if you need me" he left a message on James phone. Hayden opened the limo's door and slid into the backseat closing the door behind him "we're going to Slaps Bed & Breakfast" he told Ravi. Ravi backed the limo out of the parking lot of Canna Striata Gardens and onto Route 7 heading west.

James and Matt was going through Terry's files, Matt looked at the floppy-disk "how are we going to see what's on this" Matt asked James, suddenly a message came through James phone, James looked to see who it was, it was Hayden, James listened to the message and then hung up his phone. James started putting back the file into the folder "what are you doing" Matt asked him "come on we're going to Marks 1 Variety" he told Matt. Matt was considering leaving the floppy-disk behind "bring that with you, lets go" James told him as he left the conference room, Matt slid the floppy-disk in the back pocket of his pants and followed behind James. When they got into James Escalade Matt took the disk out of his pants pocket and put it on the vehicle's dashboard "I still don't know how we're going to see what's on that" Matt said to James "we'll figure it out when we get there" James replied. "Where are we going" Matt asked James "Marks 1 Variety on Kamper, 1751 Kamper Avenue the GPS is telling me" James replied "I know that place, that's a nice neighborhood" Matt said "an abandon car was found there early this morning" James told him "do we know who's car it is" Matt asked him "right now our job is to find out if the cashier there has any valuable information for us" James replied as he started up the Escalade, he drove out of the underground parking and onto Tankanak Circle, the JBI building in Brookshore is located at 1 Tankanak Circle. They were going southeast so James took Silvercreek Road which was pretty much a main road in Brookshore, it went from north Brookshore to southeast Brookshore, it's so long that it goes by two major malls in Brookshore. It took James just over ten minutes to get to Kamper

Avenue, he made a right turn onto Kamper. "The GPS shows that it's not too far up on our right" James said to Matt "I'll keep an eye out for it" Matt told him, not too long after he spotted it "here it is coming up here" he told James, James turned into the store's parking lot. The Brookshore police had already taken the Pontiac Sunfire to their lab, there was two cars parked in Marks 1 Variety's parking lot plus the escalade. James parked between the two cars and got out along with Matt, they entered into the store through a pair of glass sliding-doors. There was hardly anyone in the store just a young couple at the ATM machine making a withdrawal and a couple of middle aged men buying cold drinks and lottery tickets. James and Matt walked up to the cashier "hi my name is James Morris, Profiler for the JBI, were you working last night" James asked the young cashier as he showed him his badge "no I wasn't but Sam was" the cashier replied "where can we find Sam" James inquired "she's working in the back right now doing inventory" the cashier replied "it's through that door" the cashier added as he pointed in the direction of the door. James opened the door leading into the back, in the back looked like a small warehouse, as they walked they came upon a young lady counting boxes off a wooden pallet "hi there are you Sam" James asked the young lady "yes" she replied wondering what was going on "James Morris,

Profiler for the JBI" James said as he showed her his badge "I heard you were working last night" James asked Sam "yes that's right" she replied "did you see anything strange or out of the norm" James inquired "are you talking about what happened last night" Sam asked James "what did happen" James asked "well I saw a man standing at the phone-booth next to the store watching a lady in the store through the window" she told James "how do you know he was watching at her, he could have been on the phone" James asked her "no that phone hasn't been working for the past five years, plus when she left the store I noticed that she wasn't at her car, she was gone and so was he, all I saw was a bag of groceries on top of a car" Sam told him. "What does this man look like" Matt asked Sam "he's average built about five feet eleven inches with short dark-brown hair, no facial hair and he wore dark rimmed glasses" Sam replied, James pulled a picture of Terry Willis out of the file he was holding and showed it to Sam "is this the man you saw" James asked her "yeah could be, same facial features but this guy was much older" she replied as she looked at the picture "okay" James said and put the photo back in the file. "Is there anything else you want to tell us" Matt asked her "yeah, when the lady came in the store I saw him park across the street in a plaza" Sam told Matt "what type of car did he drive" Matt inquired "it was a dark colored Mustang early 80's or late 70's model" Sam replied "that's quite specific" James said "my boyfriend is into cars" Sam told James "well thanks for your time Sam we'll let you get back to your work" Matt said to her and shook her hand. James and Matt got back to James escalade, as they sat there in the vehicle James went through the questions he asked Sam, they were written on a notepad "I believe we have a big lead here Matt" James said to Matt "yeah I know, she ID'd the same car Terry Willis Drives" Matt replied "this couldn't be a coincidence, I think we have a suspect" James said as he started up the escalade. He backed out onto Kamper Avenue and headed back to Silvercreek Road "where are we going now" Matt asked James "we're going to meet up with Hayden at Slaps Bed & Breakfast" James replied. James made a right turn off Silvercreek Road and onto Magenta Tree Lane, he took Magenta Tree Lane south to Palm Avenue, he was planning on taken the Palm Avenue Bridge into Amaryllis Jaiz. "I wonder if Hayden found anything new" Matt asked James "I believe so, I heard from Kimberly he went to Amaryllis Jaiz because a body was discovered in Canna Striata Gardens" James replied "do you think it's the missing lady from the store on Kamper" Matt asked him "I'm not sure but we'll soon find out" James replied.

Ravi drove up the long drive way beyond the gate that lead to Slaps Bed & Breakfast, the drive way was paved with interlocking stone, it turned into a round-about in front of the building, in the center of the round-about there was a stone fountain with goldfish in it, the fountain was surrounded by palm hedging. The limo pulled up in front of Slaps Bed & Breakfast, there were two police cruisers parked in front of them, Hayden got out of the limo and went to the front passenger door, Ravi opened the window "this might take a while, are you going to be okay here" Hayden asked him "I'm fine, if I get bored I can always listen to the classics" Ravi replied. Hayden found that very strange but that's Ravi "okay" Hayden said as he walked away, Hayden went to the front door opened it and went in. "Hi welcome to Slaps Bed & Breakfast" the lady at the front desk said to Hayden, he showed her his badge "is Madam Zebandee in" Hayden asked the young lady "yes she's in the lounge speaking with two police officers" she replied. Hayden left the front lobby and headed to the lounge, when he got to the lounge he saw Madam Zebandee at the bar talking with two police officers. As Hayden came closer to the them Madam Zebandee spotted him, she got off the stool she was sitting on and went over to Hayden "hey Miss" one of the officers said to her but she ignored him "for twenty minutes they've been questioning me about T" she said to Hayden as she walked closer to him "did T come by today" Hayden asked her "I already told them he got a lap dance from one of the girls early this morning" she replied "okay calm down, can you get the girl he was with" Hayden asked Madam Zebandee "yeah sure" she replied, she asked the bartender to call for Opal Rain over the building's PA system. "Madam is there anything you know about T, anything personal" Hayden asked her "I remember one time he came in he had a white plastic card clipped to his belt, I noticed written on it was Passco Regional Museum, when he seen that I saw it he took it off and put it in his pocket" Madam Zebandee told him "okay that's good information" Hayden said to her as he wrote it down in his notepad. The bartender escorted Opal to Madam Zebandee and went back to tend bar "Opal this man is a Profiler for the JBI he's going to ask you some questions so just be truthful" Madam Zebandee explained to her. Opal was a young lady of nineteen years, she had shoulder length black hair with a tawny complexion, she stood about five feet six inches in height with an athletic built, she was wearing a purple tank-top with a purple thong-bikini bottom and white sneakers. "Is this about Terry" Opal asked Hayden "why would you say that" Hayden asked her "well I just assumed he must of done something bad, he seemed a little off, very private and defensive you know" Opal explained to Hayden "he said his name was Terry" Hayden asked her "yeah he told me to call him Terry" Opal replied "anything else" Hayden asked "well when he sat down for his lap dance he took his keys out of his pants pocket and put it on the small table next to him, that's how I knew he drove a Mustang, he promised to take me for a drive in his Mustang, he also had an I.D card from the Passco Regional Museum" she told Hayden with a smile. "Okay that's great, thank you for your time" Hayden said to Opal as he wrote down what she told him "back to work" Madam Zebandee told Opal and gave her a few slaps on her exposed bottom, Opal skipped away from Madam Zebandee's touch "ow ow ow" she giggled. Hayden's cell phone began to ring "excuse me" Hayden said to Madam Zebandee as he answered it "Hayden" he answered, it was James, James informed Hayden that Terry Willis's dad was a taxidermist that died back in 1996, at the time he lived at 1278 south Route 96 with his twenty-seven year old son Terry, he also told Hayden that he was just around the corner and he was coming to meet him "okay thank you" Hayden replied and hung up the phone. "Madam I have to go, I'll have two officers here just in case T comes back" Hayden told Madam Zebandee "okay" she replied Hayden headed back to the limo. As Hayden got back into the limo he was thinking, Terry connected to the museum in Brookshore and his dad was a taxidermist 'I wonder if Terry learned taxidermy from his father' he thought. Hayden gave Lorne a call "Lorne The Wizard at your service"

Lorne answered "hi Lorne it's Hayden, I need you to dig up all you can on a Terry Willis born May 12th 1969" Hayden told him "I sure will sir, you'll have it in twenty minutes" Lorne replied. Hayden sat in the limo and looked up the Passco Regional Museum on his laptop, he was waiting for James to show up, according to James he was just around the corner. Passco Regional Museum's website came up on the laptop's screen, it said that it was located in central Brookshore at the intersection of Silvercreek Road & Lilac Trail, the website showed its address as 167 west Lilac Trail. Hayden could see through the back window James's escalade coming up the driveway, it parked behind the limo and James and Matt got out and headed for the front door of Slaps Bed & Breakfast, before they got there the rear-window of the limo went down and Hayden called them over. James and Matt walked over to the open window, the door opened up and Hayden came out of the limo "hey guys how's it going" he said to James and Matt "we went to Marks 1 Variety and spoke to someone that might of seen the killer, why I say that is that she didn't witness the actual crime" James told Hayden "did you show her a picture of Terry" Hayden asked him "the picture I have is from 1994, but I did show it to her and she said it could be him but the guy was much older and wore glasses" James replied "I believe we're on the right trail, there's just a few more things to investigate" Hayden said. Hayden heard his laptop give off a musical tone, that meant an e-mail was coming in for him "I'm here because I believe the person the Madam here knows as T is actually Terry Willis, a few minutes ago I mite have confirmed it" Hayden told James and Matt "what do you want us to do" Matt asked Hayden "head over to the police lab in Brookshore, they have Dana Hollinger's car there, we need to bring it to our lab for processing" Hayden told Matt and James "where are you going" James asked Hayden "I'm heading to the Passco Regional Museum in central Brookshore, it sounds like Terry mite of worked there recently" Hayden replied "yeah I know the place" Matt said. James and Matt headed back to their vehicle, Hayden got back into the limo, he picked up his laptop off the seat and rest it on his lap. He looked at the e-mail message that was sent to him, it was from Lorne, the e-mail was a five page information-sheet on Terry Norman Willis, it said that his father was Alvin J Willis, DOB: August 30th 1939, he worked as a taxidermist for thirty-five years at the Caiman Lodge in Beryl Rado and occasionally at his home in Umni. It stated his address as 1278 south Route 96 in Umni, something on the information-sheet got Hayden's attention, after Alvin's death in 1996 his will was read, it stated in the will that the house in Umni at 1278 south Route 96 was to be giving to his son Terry 'this is good now we have where he lives' Hayden thought to himself. "Where to sir" Ravi asked Hayden "Passco Regional Museum" Hayden replied without looking up from the computer screen, Ravi started up the limo and headed down the driveway and onto Route 9. He took highway 33 into Brookshore, Hayden also saw on the information-sheet that Terry started working at the Passco Regional Museum on March 11th 2006, he was laid off on October 2nd 2019, technically he was relieved of his position, Terry made some of the female staff at the museum uncomfortable, there was also an incident in the ladies change-room at the museum. Hayden could see that Terry's position at the museum was a taxidermist, he knew right then that he was on the right trail and that Terry was most likely his killer. The information-sheet also stated that Terry's present address was 1278 south Route 96, Hayden thought it wouldn't hurt to send a couple of uniformed officers there to see if he's home. Hayden called the Umni Police Department, a Captain Ogammi answered "Umni police Ogammi here" he said, Hayden told him who he was and the reason for his call, he also told him to send two uniforms out to 1278 south Route 96, Ogammi complied. "Should we be worried up here" Ogammi asked Hayden "now that we know where he lives I'm confident that we'll have this wrapped up pretty soon" Hayden replied "well agent if you need any help you know where I am" Ogammi told him "thank you" Hayden said and hung up the phone.

It was now nighttime in Brookshore, thirty-eight year old pharmacist Leann Greggs was finishing up for the day at Gray Sparrow Drugs Store, she was also waiting for a friend to pick her up, they were going out for a couple beers. A week ago Leann cot her then boyfriend cheating on her with another lady so her friend promised to take her out to get her mind off of him. Leann heard a car horn, she went outside and locked the store's door behind her, her friend pulled up in front of her in a blue 2001 CRX. "Hey Chris how you doing" Leann asked as she slid into the car's front passenger seat "I'll be better once we get to the bar" Chris replied, Chris's name was actually Christine but anyone that knew her just called her Chris for short. "We're not going man-hunting are we" Leann asked Chris "no only for a couple beers and a bite to eat if you want to" Chris replied "okay because I just broke up with Dave a week ago" she told Chris "I know" Chris replied. Leann noticed that for a few blocks a black car was following them "turn left up here" she told Chris "why" Chris asked her "please just do it" Leann told her "okay fine" Chris complied and turned left on Shear Diamond Street. Leann looked through the rear view mirror and saw that the black car kept going straight "what was that about" Chris asked her "nothing I guess I just thought we were being followed" she replied. Chris turned left onto Filmore Lane "where are we going" Leann asked her "we're going to Turtle's Tavern" Chris replied "that place is too busy and too loud" Leann told her "I know but you need to get your mind off of Dave, this break-up is stressing you out and making you paranoid" Chris said to her "don't worry we won't stay long" Chris added "okay only if you promise that we won't stay long" Leann said "I promise" Chris replied. It didn't take them too long to get to Turtle's Tavern, the parking lot at Turtle's was full, there was only a couple parking spots left. Chris pulled into a parking spot next to a black Mustang and put her car in park, they both got out of the car and headed into Turtle's. Inside Turtle's was fairly spacious, as they came into the front door there was a bar to their left, in front of the bar there were stools with people sitting on them, to their right were tables and booths that were occupied by customers, at the back was a dance-floor with a jukebox in the corner. Leann and Chris sat down at the end of the bar on two vacant stools, behind the bar was a big screen TV that was showing a baseball game, there was also two small TV's mounted on the wall behind the bar that you could play trivia on. "It's nice in here" Leann said to Chris "see I told you, this will help you get your mind on something positive" Chris told her, the bartender came over to the two women "what can I get for you ladies" the bartender asked them "two Blue Toucans please" Chris replied "coming right up" the bartender said and them left to get their drinks. "have you moved into your new place yet" Chris asked Leann "yeah I moved in a couple days ago" Leann replied "so tell me, how do you like it" Chris inquired "it's cozy it's a one bedroom apartment, yeah I like it" Leann replied "that's good how do you like the neighborhood" Chris asked her "I've only been there two days, give me some time to get to know the place" Leann told her "anyways I'm happy for you" Chris replied. The bartender came back with the ladies drinks "here you go" the bartender said as he placed the two bottles of beer on the bar in front of them "do you ladies want a menu" the bartender asked them "no we're okay for now" Chris replied "okay well I'm here if you need me" the bartender told her and then left to tend to other customers. Leann and Chris sat there drinking their beers "there's a lot of handsome men in here" Chris said as she looked around the tavern "what about your husband" Leann asked her "I'm not doing nothing it's just flirting" Chris replied "yeah but I don't think Ken would appreciate that" Leann said to her "what he doesn't know won't hurt him" Chris told her. Leann laughed at Chris's remark "you're unbelievable" Leann said to her "oh come on I'm not thinking about going to bed with anyone" Chris replied. Chris finished her beer and asked the bartender for a Coke "no more beer" he asked her "I'm driving" she told him "but you can get my friend one more when she's finished" Chris added "sure thing" the bartender said and then went to get Chris her drink. Chris turned and faced Leann "you know sooner or later you're going to have to find a new boyfriend" she told her "right now I need some time to myself" Leann said "just remember you're not getting any younger" Chris reminded her "thanks for reminding me" Leann replied sarcastically "I'm just saying" Chris said. The bartender came back with a glass-cup and a can of Coke, he set the cup on the bar in front of Chris and then opened the Coke, he poured the Coke into the glass and stopped before it got to the top then placed the almost empty can of Coke beside the glass "thank you" Chris said to him "enjoy" he told her as he answered the ringing phone that was behind the bar. "that's a neat looking dance floor" Leann said to Chris "yeah Saturday nights they have dance competitions and you can win prizes" Chris told her, a middle aged man named Jacob Pilzner overheard the two ladies talking about the dance-floor, he's a local in the area he lived here all his life so he was willing to play tour-guide for the two ladies. "Sorry I just overheard you speaking about the dance-floor" Jacob said over Leann's shoulder "that's right" Leann replied as she turned her head towards him, cutting off all communication from

Chris "they also have a fancy jukebox over there, I can show you for a dance" he told her lightheartedly. Leann smiled and gazed into Jacob's brown-eyes, she saw that he was a very handsome looking man, business like, one of those men you see on TV walking on Bowling Dice Lane with a black-leather laptop-bag or briefcase in Alan's Landing "okay one dance" she said to him "hi I'm Jacob" he said to her offering his hand in friendship "Leann" she told him and shook his hand. "Who's your friend" Chris asked Leann now noticing that she no longer had her attention "oh sorry this is Jacob, Jacob this is my friend Christine" Leann introduced her new friend to Chris and they shook hands "we're just going to checkout the dance-floor" Leann added "sure, I'll be here when you come back" Chris winked at her, they got off their stools and headed to the dance-floor. When they got to the dance floor Jacob showed her the jukebox, its body was shaped like a 1950's style jukebox but inside its controls played a selection of music through an MP3 CD player, the top is encased in clear Amethyst-crystal with paisley leaf patterns on it that give off spectacular light shows as the music plays. "Your friend is right they have a dance-off here in January, third week of January I believe" Jacob said to Leann "is this a regular spot for you" Leann asked Jacob "I'm not too sure what you mean by that but if you mean am I a local, yes I live in the neighborhood"

Jacob replied "I'm sorry I didn't mean anything by that" she said apologetically "aw don't sweat it I find myself coming here quite often sometimes" he told her. Jacob slipped a Janoesian Silver-piece into the money slot of the jukebox and chose the song Shining Star by The Manhattans, he then put his hands around Leann's waist which made her feel relaxed, she rested her hands on his shoulders "something easy to dance to" he said in her ear as they started to slow-dance, couples were slowly coming on the dance-floor until the dance-floor was filled with couples dancing. After their dance Leann and Jacob was back at the bar with Chris, Leann was halfway through her second Blue Toucan "what do you do for a living" Leann asked Jacob "I'm a mechanical engineer at the Audi Plant here, lately I've been working from home because I sprained my ankle playing squash" he replied "is that the one at Magenta Tree Lane" Chris inquired "that's the one" Jacob said and finished off his bottle of Corona, he placed the empty bottle on the bar "I'm sorry I gotta get home I have an early day tomorrow" Jacob said to the two ladies, he pulled out one of his business-cards from his back pocket, it had the Audi company logo on it "here's one of my cards it has my cell number on it, you can call me anytime even if you're looking for someone to talk to" he said and handed Leann the card. "Well it was nice to meet you Jacob I hope we can do this again" Leann said, they hugged, Jacob disappeared into the crowd of standing customers at the bar as he headed towards the tavern's front door. Leann really liked him, she thought he was a nice guy with a little bit of mystery, she looked at his card and then put it in her purse "he seems like a nice guy" Chris said to her "yeah I guess" Leann replied pretending to play it off that she didn't feel a connection "it sounds like you're not going to give him a call" Chris asked using reverse-psychology "I didn't say that" Leann replied sharply. The two ladies finished up their drinks and left the tavern, out front there were no cars parked around Chris's "looks like this place is filled with just locals" Chris commented as she took her car keys out her purse, with her thumb she pressed the base of the key and the car's doors unlocked, Leann opened her side door and got in. Chris got behind the wheel and started up the CRX she backed out onto Filmore Lane and headed west to Shear Diamond Street "thanks for taking me there I had a good time" Leann said to Chris "no probs you needed it sister" Chris replied and gave her a friendly smile "and I really do think you should give Jacob a call" Chris added "I'll think about it" Leann told her. Chris turned left onto Shear Diamond Street "lets see if I remember the directions to your new pad" Chris said to Leann "you can always punch it in your GPS system" Leann told her "true but I'm going by memory here" Chris said to her "374

Barble Dove Circle right" she asked Leann "I guess we'll find out soon" Leann replied with a mysterious tone in her voice "okay sure put me to the test, I'm up for it" Chris said. When Chris turned right onto Bessy Drive from off of Shear Diamond Street a black Mustang coming from the opposite direction on Shear Diamond Street turned left onto Bessy Drive and followed behind Chris at a safe distance. Bessy Drive is a short residential road, branching off of Bessy Drive to the left is Barble Dove Circle, Chris made the left turn onto Barble Dove Circle and so did the black Mustang, Barble Dove Circle is a fair size street that went in a circle, it had mostly bungalows with some variety-stores and parkettes. "Okay we're not too far away" Chris said "very good" Leann said playfully "this is a nice neighborhood" Chris told her "you like it" Leann asked her "yeah I like it" Chris replied, Chris spotted Leann's place on the right, she parked the car on the curb in front of Leann's house. Leann got out of the car and stood next to the open passenger-side door "I would come in and check it out but it's getting late and I don't want to have Ken worrying" Chris said to Leann "Ken's probably a sleep on the couch with the TV's volume up high on the sports channel" Leann said to her "yeah probably but in any case I gotta get home it's late" Chris replied "what time is it" Leann asked her "the stereo says 11:51pm" Chris replied. Leann looked up over the top of the CRX and saw a black car about sixty feet away parked next to some ivy-hedging, it was facing them on the other side of the road, she cot when it's head-lights went off but no one came out of the car, the windows were tinted black so it was hard to see who was inside. To Leann it looked like the car she seen earlier 'it couldn't be the same car' she thought 'but what if it was' she thought into it "shut the door sister I gotta go" Chris said to her "oh sorry, drive safe" Leann told her as she shut the passenger-side door. Chris started up the car and drove off, Leann went up to her front door opened it and went in, she closed the door and locked it, it had a dead-bolt lock, she locked that to, Leann went to the living room window and peeked through the blinds, she saw that the black car was still parked outside. This was causing Leann to worry for her safety 'if it's the same car that means it's following her but why' she thought, her concern level started building, she decided to call 661 "hi this is Leann Greggs at 374 Barble Dove Circle there's a strange looking car parked outside my house I think it followed me home, I'm just really concerned for my safety can you send someone out here" she told the 661 operator, the operator told her that they have a car on route. A few minutes later a squad-car drove up her driveway and two uniformed officers got out and went up to the front door, one officer rang the door-bell. Leann was in the kitchen she went to the front door "who is it" she asked "it's the police mam" one of the officers replied, she opened up the door and saw standing in the open doorway two uniformed police officers "hi mam Officers Gatton and Jeffers, you reported seeing a strange vehicle" Officer Gatton asked "yes come in please" Leann replied. Leann escorted the officers to the kitchen where she was just sitting around the kitchen-table drinking a glass of water, she sat back down around the table "can you tell us what happened miss" Officer Gatton asked her "well I did a double shift at work yesterday and finished around 10:30pm, a friend of mine picked me up and we went for a couple drinks, on the way to where we were going to have the drinks I notice a black car following us so we turn off the street we were on and went in a different direction, we decide instead on going to Turtle's Tavern, after coming from Turtle's Tavern I see the same car parked out front of my house" she told the officer "you said the car was black, can you describe it a little more" Gatton asked her "it was like a sports car with mag tires I believe an older Mustang from the late 1970's" she replied "did you say Mustang" Gatton asked her "yes, why" she asked. Officer Gatton remembered that he seen a flyer at the station saying that the JBI is looking for a black late 70's to early 80's Mustang related in a series of murders "did you happen to see the person inside the car" Gatton asked Leann "no the windows were blacked out, why don't you just go and check for yourself" she asked them "no one's out there mam" Gatton told her, Gatton reported it in to the JBI, Special Agent James Morris took the call, while Gatton was doing that Leann went into the living room and looked through the blinds that covered the living room window, she saw nothing the car was gone. "Mam" Gatton called to Leann, she came back to the kitchen "someone will be coming by in a few minutes to speak with you farther on this matter, we'll be outside until they get here" Gatton informed her "okay" Leann said, Leann wasn't too sure what was going on all she knew is that she didn't want to be alone so it was perfectly okay with her for the police to be outside. Gatton took the report with him that he wrote down on a pad of yellow-lined paper, both officers left the house and went back to the cruiser, Leann locked back the front door after the officers left, she was still a little concerned for her safety even though the car was gone. Leann sat on the sofa in the living room and waited for whomever the police said was coming, she sat there looking through a magazine, twenty minutes later there was a knock at the door, she went to the door and opened it. At the door were two men dressed in two piece suits "hi Miss Greggs I'm James Morris a Profiler for the JBI this is my partner Matt Davis we would like to ask you a couple questions" James said to Leann as he showed her his credentials "please call me Leann, you can come in" she told them. She escorted the two agents to the living room "this is a nice place" Matt complimented "thank you I just moved in" she told him, they sat in the living room around a small mahogany center-piece, "do you live alone" James asked Leann "yes I just broke up with my boyfriend, we were going to get married" Leann replied "I'm sorry to hear that" James said to her "why are you here" she asked James "I read the police report of what happened tonight" James told her and continued "it says here you left work with a friend, where do you work" James asked her "Gray Sparrow Drugs, I'm a pharmacist" she replied "okay and from there you went to Turtle's Tavern correct" James asked her "that's only after I found out that we were being followed" Leann replied. "About how long would you say you were at Turtle's Tavern" James asked "about an hour and a half" Leann replied, James knew Turtle's Tavern he been there a couple times and he also knew that time of night the place would be packed with people. "When you got to Turtle's did you see the car again" James inquired, Leann thought about it before she answered "oh my God yes, we parked right beside it" Leann replied as she covered her mouth in shock. James leaned forward in the chair he was sitting in and placed his hand on Leann's shoulder "it's okay you're safe" he assured her "I have a picture I'm going to show you, please look at it carefully" James told her, Matt took a picture of Terry Willis out of his jacket pocket and gave it to James, the picture was giving to them by Hayden after he came back from visiting the Passco Regional Museum. James showed Leann the picture, the picture was a recent picture of Terry Willis taken a year ago "have you ever seen this man" James asked her, Leann looked at the picture "I'm not sure" she said "take your time and think back" James told her. Leann took the picture from him and studied it, then a light bulb went on in her head "yeah he was sitting at a booth in the tavern" she replied, the picture fell out of her hand and onto the center-piece "oh my God am I in danger" she asked as she started shaking and breathing heavily "no not at all mam just calm down, do you want me to get you a glass of water" Matt intervened "yes please" Leann replied as she held her chest slowly calming herself down, Matt went to the kitchen to get her a glass of water. "Miss Greggs the cruiser that's out front is going to be there when you wake up in the morning so you have nothing to worry about" James assured her "is the man in the picture dangerous" Leann asked James "right now he's someone of interest nothing more" James replied. Matt came back with a glass of water and handed it to Leann "here you go" he said "thank you" Leann replied and took a drink, James gave Leann one of his business cards "my cell-phone number is there if you think of anything new or if anything new arises feel free to give me a call" James told her. Leann looked at the card and then placed it on the center-piece "one more question Miss Greggs, what is your friend's name" James asked her "Christine Namandi" she replied "okay I guess that's it" James said as he stood up, Leann also got up out of the sofa she was sitting in and escorted James and Matt to the front door "make sure to keep your doors locked" James advised her as him and Matt exited the house, Leann shut and locked the door behind them.

Early the next day Hayden was at a coffee shop just around the corner from the JBI building, Ravi was at a car-wash across the street from the coffee shop. Hayden sat in a booth next to the shop's large window, he was sipping on a cup of hot-chocolate and going over the information-sheet Lorne had sent him. Yesterday Hayden had visited the Passco Regional Museum, he spoke with a Garret Unoaggu the museum's curator, Garret told him the reason why he hired Terry was because he was very detailed and dedicated to his work, he didn't have any detourant like a girlfriend, wife or kids. Hayden was looking for any other property that Terry owned or that his dad gave to him, Terry wasn't home when the Umni police went to his house, Hayden saw on the information-sheet that Alvin Willis owned a cabin in Beryl Rado.

Hayden's cell-phone started ringing, he answered it, it was James, he told Hayden that him and Matt was heading to Turtle's Tavern to follow up on a lead they got "okay" Hayden replied and hung up the phone.

THE CABIN

Ravi had finished cleaning the limo and he pulled up in the parking lot in front of the coffee shop, he turned off the car's engine and sat there with his window down waiting for Hayden. Hayden looked through the window and saw that Ravi was finished at the car-wash so he packed up the file in a folder he had on Terry Norman Willis and headed outside with his cup of hot-chocolate. Hayden got into the back seat of the limo "whoah! It smells great in here" he said to Ravi "yeah I did some vacuuming" Ravi replied "thank you" Hayden told him "where to sir"

Ravi asked him "I'm not too sure yet, give me a few minutes" Hayden replied.

Later on in the day around brunch James and Matt showed up at Turtle's Tavern, the place was quite empty that time of day, there was only around three or four customers sitting at the bar. James and Matt came up to the bar "hi there can I get you anything" the bartender asked them "we're here to speak with the manager" James replied "I'm the owner and manager here" the bartender told them "and apparently the bartender to" James said as he gave him a smile "that's right how can I help you" the bartender asked. "James Morris profiler for the JBI" James replied as he showed the bartender his badge "what does the Feds want with me" the bartender inquired "is there anywhere we can talk in private" James asked as he put away his badge "yeah one second, JOY CAN YOU TAKE OVER THE BAR FOR ME" the bartender called over to one of the two waitresses on the floor. Joy came behind the bar "I have a office in the back" he told James and Matt as he pointed them in the direction of the office, James and Matt followed behind the bartender as he went to his office. When they got to the bartender's office he sat behind his desk "please have a seat" he told them, James and Matt sat in the two chairs that were in front of the desk "before we get started can I get your name" James asked the bartender "Ben Hammerlay"

Ben replied "were you working the bar last night" James asked Ben "I work the bar every night excepted for Sundays" Ben replied wondering what James was getting at, James took the picture of Terry Willis out of his jacket pocket and showed it to Ben "did you see this man here last night" James asked him. Ben took the picture from James and carefully looked at it "yeah he looks like the guy that was sitting in one of the booths on the floor, hmm" Ben replied still looking at the picture "is there something else" James inquired noticing that Ben had something on his mind "well the waitress that waited that table told me that he creeped her out and that he only ordered one beer, she said for the rest of the time he was sitting there he ignored her when she came by to ask him if he needed anything else, it was like his attention was focused elsewhere" Ben replied "has he ever been it here before" James asked "no that was the first I ever seen him" Ben replied. "Why all the questions, who is this guy" Ben asked James as he handed him back the picture "nothing to worry about it's just routine questioning" James assured Ben as he put the picture back in his jacket pocket "bullshit I think I have a right to know if someone dangerous comes into my establishment, that's it ain't it he's a dangerous person, so what did he do, kill someone" Ben asked "thank you for your time sir we'll get back to you if we have any other questions" James told Ben as him and Matt got up out of the chairs they were sitting in. "So you're not going to tell me what's going on" Ben asked James "no but I do have another question for you, why did you name this place Turtle's Tavern" James inquired "when I was in the services in training when the platoon I was in went for runs I was the one keeping up the rear so they gave me the nickname Turtle" Ben told him "hmm interesting" James said and continued "once again thanks a lot for your time we'll see ourselves out" James said to Ben and shook his hand. James and Matt left the tavern and got back in the escalade "so what do you think" Matt asked him as he shut the vehicle's door "I think he stalked that young lady" James replied.

Hayden decided on heading back to the office to speak with Lorne. When he got back to the office Lorne was in the lunch room making himself a cup of coffee, Lorne opened up the staff fridge and took out a can of whipped-cream, he sprayed some over his mug of coffee and then rested the can on the lunch room counter. "That can't be good for your blood-sugar" Hayden said to him as he watched him from the lunch room's doorway "it is but I had a late night last night" Lorne replied, Hayden and Lorne sat around one of the tables in the lunch room "Lorne I need you to dig up any information on a cabin Alvin Willis owned out in Beryl Rado" Hayden told him "sure I can do that, oh yeah before I forget a Captain Ogammi from the Umni Police Department called for you, they obtained a search warrant on the house at 1278 south Route 96 he asked if you could come up there" Lorne informed him. Hayden assumed that Ogammi must have found something so he got up out of his seat and headed back to the elevator "email me that information on the cabin" he told Lorne before he left the lunch room. Hayden took the elevator down to P2 underground parking and walked a short distance to his limo, Ravi was in the driver's seat listening to a Kelo-ball match on the radio. Hayden opened the limo's back door and slid in "who's winning" he asked Ravi as he closed the door "Hannon Dragons are up 3-1" Ravi replied "we're going to Umni, the address is 1278 south Route 96" Hayden informed Ravi "I know where that is, that's close to the marina" Ravi said to Hayden as he started up the limo. Ravi backed the limo out of it's parking spot, he headed up the parking lot's ramp and onto Tankanak Circle, he was planning on taking the PBP into Umni. The Kelo-ball game was still playing on the limo's radio "so do you think Alan's Raiders are going to win the cup" Hayden asked Ravi "it's hard to say sir but if I was to guess I think the Tamerra Bullhorns have a pretty good chance this year" Ravi replied. It didn't take them too long to get to Umni and the address wasn't that far from the PBP, Ravi exited off the PBP onto Route 40, he headed west on Route 40 until he got to Route 96 and made another left turn onto Route 96. Route 96 bent slightly to the east and went under the PBP ending at Mollymawk Marina, Hayden spotted the house on his right "there it is" Hayden told Ravi as he pointed in the direction of the house. Ravi parked across the street from the house, Hayden could see that there were a few police cruisers parked out in front of the house and a mobile crime lab van parked in the driveway. "I shouldn't be too long" Hayden told Ravi and got out of the limo, Hayden walked up the driveway to the front door, the front door was open with a uniformed police officer standing in front of the doorway. Hayden got to the front door and showed the officer his badge, the officer let him in "where can I find Captain Ogammi" he asked the officer "he's in the kitchen" the officer replied as he pointed towards the kitchen. As Hayden made his way to the kitchen he saw crime scene investigation people in white jump-suits carrying large brown-paper bags filled with stuff out to their mobile crime lab. When he got to the kitchen Captain Ogammi was standing in front of an open cupboard filled with clear glass jars that had in them a human body parts, either a tongue, ear or severed hand etc, they were soaking in formaldehyde. Hayden walked up to Ogammi "Captain Ogammi I presume" Hayden said as he held out his hand in a greeting gesture, Ogammi turned to see Hayden standing beside him "just call me Dean" Ogammi told him, they shook hands "Hayden Alexander JBI Profiler" Hayden said "well Hayden have you ever seen anything like this" Dean asked him "truthfully, yes a few years back" Hayden replied. Dean gave Hayden a strange look "I guess you federal boys seen all manner of things" he said to Hayden "not all of us" Hayden replied, Hayden didn't want to lock horns with Dean he knew that this was now a JBI case "look this guy has dropped bodies in three different cities, I'm not here to step on anyone's toes we need help from all three police departments on this" Hayden told Dean "okay well we came here yesterday and no one was home but we detected a strong odour coming from the house so we secured a search-warrant with a judge and here we are" Dean informed him. Hayden now looking around the kitchen "what are in those brown-bags they're taken out" he asked Dean "human limbs we found in the master-bedroom closet" Dean replied "this is a regular horror-shack" Dean added sarcastically. The smell was very strong so Dean gave Hayden some cream to wipe under his nose to help him bare the scent "once CSI finishes dusting and lifting fingerprints I need a copy of the final report" Hayden told Dean "sure thing we can send it to your office express-mail" Dean replied. "How many jars are here" Hayden asked Dean "close to a hundred, looks like he's been doing this for awhile" Dean replied "thing is in the living room there's no body parts just stuffed animal heads and stacks of old newsprint on the floor" Dean informed him "doesn't surprise me he is a taxidermist" Hayden said. Hayden left the kitchen and went across the hall to the living room "where you going" Dean asked him "to check out what you're talking about" Hayden replied as he left for the living room, Dean followed behind him. Hayden stepped into the living room, he saw that there was stuffed animal-heads mounted on the walls, to the right of Hayden there was a cream colored leather sofa that looked to be from the 1930's, in front of him was a large Cherry-wood desk, on top of it were stacks of old newsprint, there was also stacks of old newsprint on the floor filling up the room. Hayden started looking through the newsprint, some newsprint was dated back in the 1920's others from the fifties and sixties "what are you doing" Dean asked him "why would they be saving newsprint" Hayden then asked Dean "what are you getting at" Dean inquired "well I don't think Terry collected all these prints he wasn't born until 1969, some of these are dated from the 30's" Hayden replied "what do you plan on doing with these" Dean asked him "maybe in studying these prints we can find a core to what made him who he is" Hayden told him. Dean gave Hayden an odd look and then a slow-smile "aw, right you're a profiler, you guys study behavior, try to get in his head right" Dean said with a little farce in his tone "how else do you think I found out where he lives" Hayden replied. Dean looked around the living room at all the animal-heads displayed like trophies on the walls "so I guess we'll have to fingerprint everything" Dean said to Hayden "for starters, yeah" Hayden replied "I have a feeling it's going to be a long day" Dean said "I'll have a few of my men come here and transfer these newsprint to the JBI lab" Hayden informed him. Hayden's cell-phone started ringing, it was Lorne "excuse me Captain I have to answer this call" Hayden said to Dean as he stepped out into the front hallway "sure, do your thing" Dean replied. "Hayden speaking" he said into the phone, Lorne told him that he had a address for Alvin's cabin in Beryl Rado, he also informed Hayden that Terry Willis goes there once a week to pick up mail and that there's a pond near the cabin where Terry liked to hang out when he was a boy, he also emailed Hayden information on the cabin "thank you Lorne" Hayden said "anything else just give me a ring" Lorne replied and hung up the line on his end. Hayden headed back into the living room "I just realized that the eyes on the animal-heads mounted on the walls are human" Dean informed Hayden as he came into the living room "hmm" Hayden said to himself as he walked up close to the stuffed head of a east African black-panther, he stood in front of the head and stared into it's blank eyes "yes you are right Dean" he said to Captain Ogammi "what do you make of that" Dean asked him "well it's certainly odd behavior" Hayden replied with some farce "this thing is really twisted" Dean said. Hayden had an hunch, he called Major Byron Phelps and told him to check Dee-dee Simmons and Ann Miller's body and see if the eyes are real, Byron complied and told him that he would call the medical examiner as soon as he got off the phone with him "thank you Byron I appreciate it" Hayden told him and hung up the phone. "I can hear the bells going off up there" Dean said symbolically to Hayden "sorry, pardon, oh yeah just got a hunch" Hayden replied "oh I had one of those before" Dean said fishing for the right answer. "Captain I'm heading out to Beryl Rado for a bit, I thank you for your help and keep doing what your doing, you do great work" Hayden told Dean as he patted him on the shoulder "thank you" Dean replied, Hayden headed out the front door and across the street to his limo, he opened the back door of the limo and slid onto the soft leather of the back seat. Hayden was planning on checking his email to see the information Lorne sent him, he took out his laptop-bag from a mahogany-consul in front of him, he took the laptop out of the bag and rested it on his lap. Hayden turned on the laptop with the touch of a button, the screen came on and the JBI symbol came up on the center of the screen. In his message center he opened the message Lorne just sent him, it was a six page information-sheet on a cabin in Hickory Hills, Beryl Rado that was won by a twenty-six year old Burt Willis in a card-game in 1933, Terry Willis's grandfather, the second last page on the information-sheet was a deed. Hayden read through the information-sheet, it stated that the cabin was located at 21 west Route 47 in a part of Beryl Rado they call the Hickory Hills, Hayden read further down the sheet. The sheet stated that Terry's grandfather Burt gave the cabin to Terry's dad Alvin before he died on his death-bed in 1967, Terry's grandfather Burt went into a cold-sweat and fainted at a department store with his wife at his side, when the ambulance came they brought him to the hospital, he spent five years bedridden suffering from nerve and joint pain until he died on April 22nd 1967. Hayden kept reading, he read until he got to a part that struck his interest, in 1992 Alvin added to his will that he wanted his son Terry to have the cabin in Beryl Rado, in 1994 he signed over the deed to the cabin to his son Terry "bingo! I got you" Hayden said to himself with confidence "where are we heading to now sir" Ravi asked Hayden "21 west Route 47, it's in Beryl Rado" Hayden replied "okay but we have to stop at a gas station first to fill up, that's quite a distance away" Ravi said "what's wrong Ravi you don't like road-trips" Hayden asked him "yeah I'm fine with it, just letting you know it's going to take just under an hour to get out there" Ravi explained "I'm fine with it, maybe we'll even grab a bite to eat when we're out there" Hayden told him. Down the road in Umni Ravi pulled into a Oil/Mar gas station "can you get some drinks also" Hayden asked him as Ravi got out of the limo, Hayden handed him a fifty Rupee bill (which is the same as fifty dollars) "yes sir" Ravi replied as he shut the car's door and headed up to the variety-store that was connected to the gas station. Hayden knew that Beryl Rado was a small place, they didn't have much of a police force, only a few Forest-Rangers, he would need to call Pearles Police Department and let them know to get a couple cruisers out there so that's what he did. Hayden took out his cell-phone and called the Pearles Police Department, his phone started ringing "hello Stella Xavier Pearles Police Department" a Colonel Stella Xavier answered "hi Stella" Hayden said "that voice sounds familiar" Stella said wondering who it was "it's Hayden" he replied "Hayden" she asked not too sure if she knew a Hayden "Hayden Alexander from sociology class" Hayden replied "oh right how you been" she asked him. Hayden knew Stella from back in university and when she was a rookie cop "I'm now Special Agent Hayden Alexander for the JBI" Hayden told her and continued "I'm on a very important case right now, I need you to send a couple of your cruisers over to this address, 21 west Route 47 in Beryl Rado" he instructed her "okay I'll send a couple out there right now, can I ask why" she said to him "I just sent you a picture of the suspect to your office's email, send it out and tell your men to be on the lookout for him, he drives a black Mustang" Hayden informed Stella "okay will do, where will you be" she asked him "I'm on my way to that address right now" he told her "I'll see you when you get here" she said and hung up on her end. Pearles Police Force police all of Beryl Rado considering that half of Beryl Rado falls in the Edward Region and the other half in the Southern Black Forest Region. In the Southern Black Forest Region the police in Pearles team up with the Forest Rangers to keep that region safe. Ravi came back to the limo with a plastic-bag filled with snacks and drinks, he passed it through the open window to Hayden "thank you kindly friend" Hayden said as he received the plastic-bag, he put the bag down on the seat beside him and took out of it a can of Coke. Hayden opened the can and took a drink, he then put the can in the center consul beside him. Ravi was outside putting gas in the limo for their road-trip to Beryl Rado, he figured the fastest route to take is Route 45 that would take them through Martin's Grove and then through Blainz a hamlet just east of Beryl Rado, he finished filling up the limo and screwed the gas-cap back on, he then hung up the gas spout and went around to the driver's side. Ravi opened the door and slid in behind the wheel, he shut the door and started up the limo "do you want something to drink, here" Hayden said to Ravi as he handed him a bottle of Sprite "thank you" Ravi said and took the bottle and put it in the center consul beside him. Ravi drove back out onto Route 40 and headed west until he got to Route 90, he then went south on Route 90 to Route 45 just outside of Brookshore. Right now they were on Route 45 between south Umni and Blainz about three miles northwest of Martin's Grove a suburb of Brookshore, the road was a two lane road going through rolling hills, plush green meadows and farmland. Hayden went over the information-sheet for the second time, he was looking for anything that would tell him why Terry became the person he is. Hayden thought that it might be his home-life with his relatives 'maybe something happened to him when he was a boy' Hayden thought to himself, he opened up a mahogany cabinet that was to the left of him in the limo, it was a small compartment big enough to store the bag of snacks an that's what he did but not before taken out a pack of salt roasted Planter's Peanuts 'something to munch on' he thought to himself. Hayden closed the door to the cabinet and went back to his laptop, he thought that 'maybe it would be good to have a unit sitting on his cabin, if he's not there that's where he goes to pick up his mail, he's bound to show up sooner or later'. Hayden was starting to see quite a few rock formations off to the side of the road with wild animals perched on them "it's nice and pure up here" he said to Ravi "yes sir, soon we're going to need a Humvee" Ravi replied sarcastically, Hayden chuckled at Ravi's comment "no we're fine just keep on the main road" Hayden told him "but it is beautiful out here" Hayden added "you're in the foothills right now sir" Ravi told him. Ravi could now see the sign reading Village of Blainz off to the right, Route 45 veered to the right and ran straight through Blainz (it was the only main road in Blainz) and onto Route 81 in southeast Beryl Rado, it didn't take them long at all to drive through Blainz. Ravi stopped at a rest-stop at the intersection of Route 49 and 81, they were parked next to a Village Opening which is a coffee-shop slash variety store, most Village Opening's are open 24/7 "where are you going" Hayden asked Ravi as he watched him exit the limo "I need to use the washroom, I won't be long" Ravi replied as he closed the door and headed into the Village Opening. This was the first time Hayden had been out in the country in a long while, he sat in the limo and looked through the window at a group of White-tailed deer and Sambar deer walking along the dirt shoulder of Route 49 'not something you see often in Brookshore' he thought to himself. Hayden was a city-boy, lived most his life in Alan's Landing he just moved to Brookshore six years ago, he never had the time to enjoy the outdoors. Ravi came back to the limo "sorry sir I had to use the washroom" he apologized to Hayden as he opened the door, slid in and shut it "no problem if you gotta go you gotta go" Hayden replied "there's plenty of wildlife up here" Hayden said to Ravi "oh yes we're very close to the Black Forest" Ravi told him as he started up the limo "have you been to Beryl Rado sir" he asked Hayden "no this is my first excursion up here" Hayden replied "not to worry the only thing you have to look out for is Caiman alligators, there's quite a few of them out here" Ravi informed Hayden "it sounds like you speak from experience" Hayden asked him "well I did my Young Rangers training here plus about eight years ago I was seeing a lady from Pearles" Ravi replied. "I never knew you had a rugged frontier-man side, have you ever been rock-climbing" Hayden asked him "couple times, it's hard on the joints though" Ravi said. Hayden got back to his research, Ravi drove west on Route 49 until he got to south Route 2, he made a right turn on Route 2 and headed north on 2 to Route 47. Beryl Rado didn't have much of a downtown just three intersections, it had a lot of creeks and ponds most people came there to fish and camp, there wasn't much else to do there, there are a few bike-trails so I guess if you like mountain-biking you can do that to. Beryl Rado has the most caiman attacks in all of Janoesha Harbour, they have signs posted in town cautioning visitors and the locals of caiman alligators in the area, Hayden actually just saw one walking on the shoulder of the road it then crawled off into the bushes "wish I had a camera" he said to himself. "We're almost there sir, the GPS says five minutes" Ravi informed Hayden, Ravi was now traveling west on Route 47 which was a very rural road that went through dense woodland, Hayden could hear various animals up in the trees and in the bushes, to him it sound like the petting-zoo at Hubber's Lake, although the petting zoo didn't have monkeys. "Here we go, GPS says it's on the left" Ravi said to Hayden, Hayden took a look through the windshield and saw up the road two Pearles Police SUVs "yeah it's right here on the left" Hayden told him. Ravi parked on the dirt shoulder of the road in front of one of the SUVs next to a bunch of Bindweed that has grown over a white-picket fence, Hayden got out of the limo, he shut the door and went up to the front-door window that was open "I shouldn't be too long" he told Ravi "I'll be right here drinking my Sprite" Ravi replied. Hayden headed up the driveway of Cabin 21, in it's driveway was a Pearles Police-van, on west Route 47 there was eight cabins all numbered from twenty to twenty-seven. Hayden came up to the open front door of the cabin, there was a young police officer standing there "can I help you" the officer asked Hayden, Hayden showed him his badge and the officer let him in. Inside the cabin was a large open space with a bedroom off to the left and a kitchen to the right, Hayden saw that there were officers looking through a desk and cabinet in what Hayden presumed to be the living room. An athletic looking black lady wearing a Pearles Police uniform came out of the bedroom "all the way up to the JBI I see" she said to Hayden "how are you Stella" he said to her with his arms out-stretched ready to give her a hug but she held out her hand and they shook hands instead "I am now Mrs. Stella Xavier" she informed him "it's been a while, how you been" she asked him. Hayden's head was well wrapped around this Terry Norman Willis thing that he couldn't focus on anything else "was anyone home when you got here" he asked Stella "if there was they'd be in cuffs in the back of one of the SUVs out front" she replied sharply, Hayden gave her a subtle-smile "what's going on agent, what am I looking at here" she asked Hayden "hopefully the end of this" he replied "don't you think that I have a right to know who comes into my jurisdiction" she asked him "so I'm assuming he wasn't home, I will tell you this his name is Terry Norman Willis, please don't mention this to the press" he replied "okay I can work with that" Stella said "Kimberly Anrhime my Communications Liaison has been really good at keeping this out of the media in Passco Region" Hayden told Stella "don't worry I'll make sure nothing leaks out to the press" she assured Hayden. "Okay so what's going on here" Hayden asked her "well I sent a couple units here like you asked me to, they reported that a strong odour was coming from the cabin so we proceed to enter with caution and this is what we came upon" she informed him as she escorted him to the bedroom. In the bedroom there was the dead body of a young lady with her hands and feet hand-cuffed to the bed-post, her eyes were scooped out of her head, she was completely naked her vaginal area was torn wide open with black metal specks sprinkled on it. "It looks like she's been there for at lease a couple weeks" she said "yeah it sure does" Hayden said as he moved in closer to the bed to examine the body "not a good place to leave a dead body, this time of year Beryl Rado is mild and damp" Stella said "is there a medical examiner coming" Hayden asked her "yeah they're on their way, they're probably out front right now" Stella replied, just then two men from the coroner's office came in the front door with a gurney and took the body. "It's going to be hard to get an ID off of that" Stella said "this is the second time I've missed him, no more being behind him, time to get ahead of him" Hayden told Stella "are you saying that your guy did this" Stella inquired "I need all hands on deck with this one" Hayden asked Stella "okay I'm with you" she replied instinctively "I believe he'll head back here soon, before he goes anywhere else so I need a team of your men here hiding out in the bushes and waiting for his arrival" Hayden said "I can put together a team of six men with two of them sharp-shooters" Stella offered "I only need five with one sharp-shooter" Hayden told her. Hayden's phone started ringing he answered it, it was James, one of his leads went missing a Leann Greggs, he told Hayden that him and Matt was going to checkout what's going on "okay keep me informed" Hayden told him and hung up the phone, he put it back in the inside pocket of his jacket "who was that" Stella asked him "just a fellow team member" Hayden replied "I'm going to need a copy of the coroner's report as soon as it comes out" he added "you'll have it on your desk in twenty-four hours" she assured him.

James got a call in his office from a Christine Namandi a friend of Leann Greggs, she told him that she was suppose to pick-up Leann at her house for 5:00pm, she showed up five minutes early and waited around for twenty minutes but Leann didn't show up. Christine decided on calling Leann's workplace then, but when she called the clerk working the evening shift said that she left. "Did you try her cell-phone" James asked her "yes I've tried that four different times, it only goes to voice-mail" Christine replied in a frustrated voice "okay calm down, stay where you are I'm heading out there right now" James advised her as he grabbed his keys off his desk. Right now James and Matt were on their way to Leann Greggs house to meet her friend Christine, James had turned onto Shear Diamond Street "could she have went to pay some bills that she forgot to on a previous day" Matt asked James "I don't know, something doesn't feel right" James replied. James made a right turn on Bessy Drive "I'm wondering if I should have had a squad-car following her" James said to Matt "what about the cruiser at her house" Matt asked James "they don't follow her to work" James replied "then he probably took her between work and home" Matt said "lets hope not" James replied as he made a left turn onto Barble Dove Circle. They parked on the street in front of the house, Christine's CRX was in the driveway and Christine was sitting on the front porch steps, James and Matt got out of the escalade and headed up the driveway to the house. Christine stood up as soon as she seen James and Matt walking towards her "I kept calling her but no answer, I'm worried that something happened to her" Christine said with frustration still in her voice as she approached James "okay calm down she mite have an important reason to turn off her phone" James told her "but she never does that" Christine told James "were you guys planning on going out this evening" Matt asked her "she wanted to go shopping for somethings for her house, she just moved in" Christine replied "yeah I know she did mention that" Matt said "we were going to go to Grand Mall" she told Matt. "Did you call the police" James asked her "the first thing I did was call 661" Christine replied "okay that's good, now the police is out there looking for her, don't worry they'll find her" James assured her "I'm just scared that something awful happened to her" Christine said as she started crying, Matt held her in his arms "no you can't think that way" he said doing his best to comfort her. James phone started ringing "excuse me one second I have to answer this" he told Christine as he walked away from where they were standing on the front lawn, the call was from Kimberly Anrhime, she informed James that a call came through to the phone in the conference-room from a Captain Dean Ogammi of the Umni Police Department, she said that Ogammi said that they found a body just outside The Palms Golf Course and the ID next to the body says that she's thirty-eight year old Leann Greggs from Brookshore, Janoesha Harbour. "Okay thank you Kim" James said and hung up the phone, he put it back in his pants pocket and headed back to where Matt and Christine was standing "mam something of extreme importance has come up but if you give me a call later I will be more than happy to speak with

you, for now we should let the police do their jobs"
James told her as he handed her one of his business-
cards "thank you" Christine said to James and Matt
"you're very welcome mam, stay safe" Matt told her
as they made their way back to the escalade. James
and Matt got in the vehicle and shut the door, James
started it up and drove off "where are we going" Matt
asked James "we're going to Umni" James replied
"okay, why" Matt inquired "I just received a call from
Kim she said that a Captain Dean Ogammi from the
Umni Police Department called, they found a body
just outside The Palms in Umni" James explain "do
they know who it is" Matt asked "they found an ID
card next to the body, it's Leann Greggs, they want
me up there to make a final identification of the
body" James replied. "Why did he bring her all the
way out there" Matt asked "I don't know, truthfully
we don't even know if he done this" James replied as
he took Kamper Avenue to the PBP "are you serious,
who else could it be" Matt said sharply "we don't
know if she's been murdered, they just said that they
found a body" James told Matt. It took James about
twelve minutes to get to the Route 40 exit off the
freeway, he took Route 40 west to Route 86, The
Palms golf course was located at 1210 Route 35,
actually going by its size it takes up four and a half
blocks so the address fluctuates depending on who
you ask in Umni but the front entrance is on Route

35. James turned right on Route 86 "you ever been golfing" James asked Matt "yeah I actually came here a couple times, both times I played a Back 9" Matt replied "wow! Are you good at it" James asked him "not really, fifty fifty I guess" Matt replied "here we are Route 35" James said as he made a left turn on Route 35 "look for the club-house entrance it's on your side" James told Matt. Matt looked out the window, looking to spot the front entrance to the golf course "here it is coming up" he told James as he saw the sign on the club-house saying The Palms, James turned right down the gated driveway of the golf course, he parked the escalade in front of the club-house. An officer greeted them out front as they got out and shut the doors to the escalade "hi you must be Agent James Morris I'm Officer Avers I'll be taking you to the crime-scene" Avers said to James "great after you officer" James replied. Avers brought them to the southwest section of the golf course, just over the fence from the fifteenth hole in a patch of Traveler Palm trees and Dwarf, Super Purple plants laid a woman's body, James could see that the body was naked "hi I'm Captain Ogammi" a man came up to James and greeted himself "that will be all Avers" Ogammi said, Officer Avers excused himself "where's the other guy I was expecting him" Ogammi asked James "he was called off on another assignment" James told him "can I see the body" James asked

Ogammi "yeah sure it's right over here" Ogammi escorted James and Matt over to where the body was "do you know her" Ogammi asked James "yeah that's Leann Greggs" James replied. James stooped down to get a better look at the body, the coroner was standing by waiting with a gurney for the JBI to take a look at the body and then when they were satisfied they would take the body. James could see that her head was almost decapitated, he checked her vaginal area and saw black metal specks on it "yeah it's our guy" James said to Matt, Matt just exhaled as if he had held his breath for a while and shook his head. "Are you talking about Terry Willis" Ogammi asked James "we need this to be kept out of the press understood Captain" James told him "I understand, your partner was very adamant about that also" Ogammi replied. James took a look at her hands "what's this black stuff under her fingernails" James asked Ogammi "not too sure looks like motor-oil mixed with dirt" Ogammi replied "who discovered the body" James asked "couple city-workers, Pruners that work seasonal, came back here to tend to the trees and soften up the dirt with a rake and that's when they seen her" Ogammi replied. The coroner took the body "I need a copy of the coroner's final report" James told Ogammi "I can send it to you express-mail" Ogammi informed James "the workers that discovered the body where are they now" James asked Ogammi "they're sitting in the restaurant section of the club-house, one of them seem pretty shaken up" Ogammi replied "may we speak with them" James asked Ogammi "sure! you can give it a shot" Ogammi replied.

Hayden had rented a room in a motel in town for the night, he wanted to be close by if Terry shows up, it was a upscale motel in downtown Beryl Rado named the Larimar Groves Inn, it had valet parking, a young man wearing a grey uniform offered to park the limo so Ravi handed him the keys, the room had two beds in it, it had a step-down living room with a black soft-leather couch, flat-screen TV and a white alpaca-rug on the floor "this looks nice sir" Ravi said as he brought in the room some of Hayden's work stuff that he needed. Hayden also found out that the room has WIFI and a washroom with a bathtub and shower-stall, Hayden sat down in the living room with his laptop on his lap, he was researching and creating a profile on Terry Norman Willis. There was a knock on the front door, Ravi came out of the washroom and answered it, it was the young man from the lobby "your keys sir" he said to Ravi and handed him back his keys "oh, thank you very much" Ravi said "have a nice stay sir" the young man said as he walked off towards the elevator, Ravi closed the door. Hayden was typing out a profile on Terry Willis,

Terry Norman Willis born: May 12, 1969 in Umni, Janoesha Harbour, graduated from Mollymawk High School in 1987, Hayden put down a few characteristics that he learned Terry possessed, Void of feelings, inertly complex, methodical, an eye for detail, a recluse etc. Hayden's phone started ringing, he took it out of his jacket pocket and answered it "JBI Hayden speaking, it was James letting him know that his lead Leann Greggs was found dead in Umni at The Palms "did you take a look at her eyes" Hayden asked him "no why" James asked "because I think he's removing their eyes and putting false ones in" Hayden replied "that's twisted" James said "I'm heading back to Brookshore now" James told Hayden "okay sounds good" Hayden replied and hung up the phone. 'I wonder why he's dumping bodies in random places' Hayden thought to himself.

It was late in the evening now about 7:00 the sun hadn't gone down just yet, it's orange glow was still present over the foothills of the Black Forest, Terry was heading north on Route 76 to Route 47, he had rented a room at the Lux Motel earlier in the afternoon, 'it was close enough to the cabin, if he wanted to grab his mail he can without too much travel' he thought to himself plus the heat was getting heavy in Brookshore, there were cops everywhere there. Terry was planning on chilling-out at the pond behind his cabin, he had a six-pack of Blue Toucan on the passenger-seat of his Mustang, one of them he had opened and was drinking while he sped up Route 76. He finished the bottle of beer and tossed the empty bottle out the open driver's side window "such a nice day" he said to himself with his own little rewarding smile on his face, he had his fishing-rod on the back seat 'maybe I'll do some fishing in that pond' he thought. Terry was now at the intersection of Route 76 and 48, at the northeast corner of the intersection was an alpaca-farm where they grew and groomed alpacas for their fur and meat, it's a commercial farm, it supplies malls in Brookshore, Umni and Pearles with pillows, blankets and rugs. Terry sped right by the farm, he was thinking about the pond, he named it Copper Pond because in the late afternoon when the sun is shining through the trees the reflection on the water gives it a clear-copper color. Terry could remember the first time he was at the pond, he was nine years old and his father brought him here for his birthday along with a bunch of other kids, his dad had rented a big light-blue school-bus, there was about twelve kids on the bus some boys and some girls, they were singing happy birthday to Terry, when they got to the cabin they had a barbeque and ate outside in front of the cabin, after eating some of the kids went in the cabin to play board-games, others just hung out in front of the cabin chatting with each other and there was some that went to the pond, Terry was one of them that went to the pond, it was Terry, Charlotte his next door neighbor a boy named Craig Foster who was a family friend and Jasper Dedricks his little cousin. They headed to the pond down a beaten-path that snaked through dense-bushes, Craig was up front talking and laughing with Jasper and Terry was trying his best to get comfortable around Charlotte, he had a big crush on her but was too shy to purse it or even talk to her, he tried to hold her hand and she lightly pulled away and started giggling, Terry felt awkward and the fool. "Hi my name is Terry" he finally said "Charlotte" she replied as she gave him a smile, Terry liked that his heart was beating a thousand beats a minute, he moved forward to kiss her but she backed away so he held her by the shoulders and she slapped him across the face. This made Terry angry, he punched her in the head breaking her jaw and knocking her out, at this time Craig and Jasper were already at the pond, Terry was worried about what he did and he didn't want her to tell his parents so he struck her over the head with a large rock crushing her skull, he buried the body in the banks of another pond that was close by. The next day Charlotte's parents and the people of Beryl Rado conducted a week long search for Charlotte, eventually her remains were found by an elderly couple three weeks later out in a canoe fishing, no one ever connected him to her murder. Terry smiled at that memory "sweet childhood" he said to himself as he twisted open another beer, he was coming upon Route 47, he turned right on 47 and was now traveling east on Route 47, he took a couple swigs of his beer and put the half filled bottle in the box with the others. In the distance Terry could see a couple cars parked on the side of the road, actually three of them, two on one side and one on the same side of the road he was on 'could it be people taking a leek in the bushes' he thought to himself 'no something's not right' he thought into it, Terry smelt an ambush, he stopped his Mustang in the middle of the road and waited to see what would happen. He must of waited a good five minutes and then he heard a sharp-bang sound and a half second after that there was a burning sensation in his shoulder and he was holding it as blood leaked out "FUCK!" he screamed out loud and put the car in reverse, he reversed back for about half a mile and stopped, he grabbed his Bowie-knife off the back seat, got out of the car and ducked into a dense patch of woodland nearby. Terry ran and hid in a grove of tall Fern-bushes, he strapped his Bowie-knife's sheath around his waist and put the Bowie-knife in the sheath, he could hear cars and people talking in the distance on Route 47, the only way out was to hike it through the woods before they form a grid-pattern he figured so he ripped the sleeve off his shirt and tied it around his wounded shoulder and began hiking north through the woods.

Hayden was laying on the couch resting his eyes after creating a profile on Terry Willis when his phone started ringing, he answered it, it was Stella "Agent Alexander we got him surrounded" she told Hayden, Hayden sat up in the couch "where a bouts are you" he asked her "Hickory Hills Park on Route 47 just east of Route 76, he abandoned his car on Route 47 and ran off into the park, don't worry he won't get far he's wounded and surrounded" she informed Hayden "what do you mean by wounded" Hayden asked her "one of my sharp-shooters got him in the shoulder" Stella replied "I'm on my way there right now" Hayden told her and hung up the phone. "HEY RAVI WE'RE LEAVING" Hayden called out to Ravi, Ravi came out of the bedroom "where are we going" Ravi asked "Hickory Hills Park to meet up with Stella "oh I know that place, great place to hunt deer" Ravi told Hayden "get dress we're heading out right away" Hayden said as he packed up his laptop.

Terry hiked along a dry creek-bed doing his best to shield himself from the police, the voices he heard sounded like there was a lot more than one person looking for him. Terry sat on an old tree stump under an Elm-tree, he took a look at his shoulder, his blood had totally soaked the sleeve, the bullet was still in his shoulder if he doesn't take it out soon he can die of led-poison. He heard movement in the distance, sounds of twigs breaking, Terry got up and started hiking away from the sound. He did a good twenty minutes of hiking when he came upon the edge of the Sambar Horn River and that's where he took a rest beside its clear-white rushing waters, he knelt there scooping up the water in his cupped-formed-hand and drinking it, he also put some on his wounded shoulder "those bastards ain't gonna get me" he told himself. He winced in pain as he checked his wound "not bad could be worst" he tried to convince himself, Terry got up and started hiking along the banks of the river, the river bent towards the northwest, Terry stayed along its bank.

Ravi turned left onto Route 47 off of Route 2, half a mile down Route 47 Hayden and Ravi saw a black Mustang sitting in the middle of the opposite lane, there were two Pearles Police SUVs parked beside it on the dirt shoulder of the road. On the opposite side of the road a Forest Ranger's SUV was parked, in front of it was a Pearles Police cruiser, sitting in the driver's seat with the door open was Stella Xavier going over a map of Hickory Hills Park with a Forest Ranger. Ravi parked the limo behind the Forest Ranger's SUV, Hayden got out and shut the door, he went around to the open driver's side window "do you have your phone on you" he asked Ravi "yeah it's right here in the center consul" Ravi replied "okay keep it charged and on, I might be going for a hike" he told Ravi "yes sir I'll do that" Ravi complied. Hayden left Ravi sitting in the limo and headed to where Stella was, the Forest Ranger standing beside Stella's cruiser spotted Hayden coming towards them, he turned and gave Hayden a staunch look. Stella looked up from the map to see what the Ranger was looking at, she saw Hayden walking towards her "I hope you had something to eat because it might be a long night, this is where it gets exciting" she said to Hayden as he came closer to her "evening Stella" Hayden replied with a gentleman's gesture "Ranger this is Special Agent Hayden Alexander of the JBI, Hayden this is Forest Ranger, Sergeant Jeff Embree" she introduced them to each other, they shook hands "okay enough with the formalities what do we have here" Hayden asked Stella "what we have is a cornered suspect" Stella replied "not to mention what we found in his car, right now I'm wait for CSI to come and process the car" she added. "What about the apprehension of Terry Willis" Hayden asked her "we have a team of Forest Rangers and police officers on his trail right now, we keep in contact by cell-phone or CB-radio" Stella informed Hayden "do you know where he's heading" Hayden inquired "right now we know that he's injured and he's looking for a way out of our dragnet" she told Hayden "don't worry my men know every inch of this park, he has nowhere to go" Jeff injected into the conversation "I have no doubt in that but I don't want anyone hurt in the process" Hayden told Jeff "well just to let you know the only way he can go is along the banks of the Sambar Horn River" Jeff informed Hayden. "Are you sure" Hayden asked Jeff "yeah that's the only way he can go if he wants to stay hidden, here look" Jeff said to Hayden as he showed him on the map that Stella was holding, "the park takes up one large block the Sambar Horn River flows into the park at the northwest section, everywhere else is surrounded by road and businesses" Jeff said as he showed Hayden on the map. Hayden saw exactly what Jeff was talking about "okay this is what I want you to do, get a JHSF team (which is the Janoesian Hostage & Special Forces) there posted waiting for him to show up" Hayden told Stella "it's already done, we're also waiting for their call to when they spot him" Stella replied.

Terry had followed the river for just over a quarter of a mile, he had lost too much blood and had to take a rest, one good thing is the sun had gone down so it was easy for him not to be seen, he could see Route 46 in the distance through some tall-grass and the trunks of Sabal Palm-trees. Terry sat there on a large rock catching his breath and seeing to his wound, the shirt-sleeve was caked in semi-dried blood so he soaked it in the river to wash out the blood, he also splashed water on his face and wounded shoulder, he tied the wet shirt-sleeve back around his wounded shoulder. He sat there looking around contemplating the best way to go 'the road is out' he thought to himself "I guess I just continue along the river" he said to himself. After sitting on the rock and mentally summing up some will-power he got up and started walking along the river again. Terry was feeling dizzy and staggering to stay on his feet so he leaned up against the trunk of a Sabal Palm-tree, at the corner of his eye he spotted something through the trees, it looked blueish grey to him until he seen it move and realized that it was a person, it looked to be a JHSF officer from Pearles. Terry was going to circle around behind him, Terry knew these woods pretty good, he kept low down next to the bushes out of the officer's night-scope as he carefully made his way closer to the officer, he hid under the dried leaf branches of a fallen Oak-tree. Terry was right behind the officer under the tree hiding in its leaves and branches, the JHSF officer was holding a M4 Colt Commando assault rifle, standard weapon for JHSF officers on Janoesha Harbour. The officer was staring through the scope of his rifle looking around the woods for Terry, when Terry saw an opening he pulled his knife out of its sheath and lunged at the officer holding him around the shoulders with his knife's blade to his throat. Terry found out real fast that the officer wasn't alone, other JHSF officers came out from behind trees and bushes "drop it" one of them told Terry "fuck you" Terry replied "toss the rifle or I'll kill you right now" Terry order the officer he was holding, the officer complied. There was a JHSF sharp-shooter perched in a tree two-hundred feet away he got on his Walkie-Talkie and radioed into Stella, he let Stella know that the suspect had taken one of them hostage, he also told her that he has him in his sights and what should he do. She gave him the okay to shoot him but not kill him, the sharp-shooter agreed and stopped radio contact. "If you kill him you won't get away with it" one of the officers told Terry "I want you to back off or I'll do it" Terry said as he held the officer in front of him shielding him from their bullets, just then Terry's left knee-cap exploded and he screamed out in pain "AW FUCK!" he cried out as he instinctively dropped the knife and held his leg where his knee-cap was, he then fell over to the ground and the officers moved in. They rolled Terry over on his stomach and hand-cuffed his hands behind his back. One of the Officers radioed into Stella "we have the suspect in custody" he told her, she told him to take Terry to the cell at the Forest Ranger Station in the southern Black Forest region and she will meet them there, the officer complied.

7

A PENNY FOR YOUR WISHES

After a medical-team bandaged up Terry's leg and gave him a couple injections in his shoulder and also bandage it up Terry was brought to a cell at the Forest Ranger Station in the southern Black Forest region. The Station looked like a very large cabin built of Mahogany-tree logs, raw stone and cement, it had a big front porch built of polished mahogany. They kept Terry in a cell there until the feds show up and decides where to transfer him, Terry wasn't a happy-camper sitting on the smooth-cement bed of the cell with his leg throbbing in pain, they gave him two injections that did nothing for the pain, he was thinking more like a bag of morphine would do it.

Stella showed up to the station before Hayden but she knew he was on his way there, she checked in with the Forest Ranger at the front desk "Colonel Stella Xavier badge number 34126" she told him as she gave him her badge to look at "okay you can go in" he told her as he gave her back her credentials "can you let them know to take Terry Willis out of his cell and bring him to interrogation-room number two please" she instructed the Forest Ranger "yes mam I'll do that right away" he complied. Five minutes later two Forest Rangers came into Terry's cell and put him in hand-cuffs, they escorted him to an interrogation-room, in the room they sat him down in a chair and hand-cuffed his hand-cuffs to a long steel-chain that was bolted to the ground "wait here" one of the Forest Rangers told him as they left the room. Terry looked around the room, the room was empty the only things in there were two chairs (one Terry was sitting in) around a table and a mirror on one of the four white-walls of the room. Stella entered into the interrogation-room, she had a mug full of coffee in her right hand as she came over to where Terry was sitting, she sat down in the chair across the table from him and placed her mug on the table in front of her "so what's your business in Beryl Rado" she asked Terry and picked up her mug taken a sip of coffee "who are you" Terry asked her grimacing in pain "my name is Stella Xavier, are you okay, you look to be in pain, no need to worry we're going to bring you to a hospital to get fixed up but before that I have a few questions for you" she replied as she took a peek at his injured leg. Terry's leg was burning in pain "this is torture you can't getaway with this" he told her "we ran the plates on your car and it says that you live in Umni, what are you doing in Beryl Rado" she asked him again "I was fishing" he replied "aw yes hence the fishing-rod on the back-seat of your car but we also found in the trunk a whole lot of blood, you want to explain that" she told him. Terry was trying to subside the pain that he was feeling by holding his wounded leg "can I at lease get a glass of water" he asked Stella "you need to answer my questions Mr. Willis, and then I can see about getting you some water" she informed him "okay! Yesterday I was with a friend and he took me deer hunting, while we were hunting he shot a deer and we put it in the trunk of my car, we were going to skin it and clean it at his place" Terry explained to her "well it'll be a few minutes yet until CSI gets back to me with a match on that blood" she told Terry. Stella took a couple more sips of her coffee "do you own a cabin in Beryl Rado" she asked Terry "no I usually rent a motel when I'm here" he replied "are you sure, think carefully" she said to him "I said I don't have a cabin in Beryl Rado" he staunchly replied "so you don't have a cabin at 21 west Route 47" Stella inquired "I said no" he replied "because if that's your place that's some sick shit, the body cuffed to the bed post" she said "what is this I'm not answering anymore questions until I speak with a lawyer" he informed Stella. Stella stood up out of the chair holding the mug in her right hand "alright then well I'm off, it'll take around forty minutes until we get your paper work sorted out for your transfer to the hospital, you have yourself a nice night Terry" she informed him as she patted him on the shoulder and made her way out the door, the door closed and automatically locked "CAN YOU GET ME SOME WATER" he shouted at her but there was no reply. Stella went back to Jeff's office Jeff was speaking with a fellow Forest Ranger when Stella barged in "he's not talking he lawyerd up" she told Jeff "okay I'll talk with you later Dan" Jeff told his fellow Ranger as Dan left out the door "yes Stella you were saying something" he said to her with a tinge of sarcasm in his tone "he'll be transferred to the hospital soon, I gotta call Hayden, can you get him back in his cell" she told Jeff "will do mam" Jeff said and got on his radio and radioed in for two Rangers to get Terry and bring him back to his cell. Stella called Hayden on her cell-phone, he picked up after two rings, she told him that Terry was going to be transferred to the hospital because he got shot in the shoulder and the leg, she also told him that she would email him the name of the hospital as soon as she knew, he told her thank you and they hung up.

Hayden headed back to the motel after purchasing a couple of Sambar-burgers for him and Ravi from a restaurant in town. When they got back to the Larimar Groves Inn Hayden got back on his laptop and Skyped Kimberly Anrhime, it rang through to Kimberly's office and she answered the Skype on her computer "sir I heard you went out to Beryl Rado, how is it" she asked him "great lots of fresh air, I called you to let you know that Terry Willis has been apprehended and is going to be transferred to the hospital, I need you to keep the details out of the press, just let them know that he's been apprehended" Hayden told Kimberly "okay I can do that, do you know what hospital he's been transferred to" she asked him "not right now I'm waiting for an email, once I get it I'll let you know" he replied. Hayden hung up his connection on Skype and started looking at the first information-sheet that Lorne sent him on Terry Willis, there was something that he thought he overlooked, on the information-sheet it stated that on Terry's tenth birthday there was a young girl eleven year old Charlotte Beaumont that went missing during his birthday party, they questioned all the kids that attended the party but no one knew where young Charlotte was, the information-sheet also stated that the last time anyone saw her she was with Terry and two other kids "could it be he started at a young age" Hayden said to himself. Hayden's cell-phone started ringing, he answered it, it was Stella, she told him that they're transferring Terry to North Brookshore General Hospital and that the hospital informed her if anyone wants to speak with him they would have to come by tomorrow morning after 9:00 "thank you" Hayden said to her and hung up the phone.

The next day a light fog was hanging over Brookshore but the sun was still shining through, casting groovy shadows on the sands of Tilliquimsara. It was around 10:30am and Terry was in a room on the third floor of North Brookshore General Hospital, the room was being guarded by the Brookshore Police, they had every exit guarded, they did this to prevent an escape or the paparazzi from getting into the hospital. Terry was laying upright in bed, his shoulder was bandaged up, the doctor had taken the bullet out of his shoulder and they put metal-pins in his leg and gave him a false knee-cap, his body still felt numb from what they injected in him to put him out. "How you feeling" Terry heard someone ask him, his vision was kind of blurry as he opened his eyes, but everything slowly started to come into focus, he saw a bronze-complexion looking man with short black-hair wearing gray-pleated dress-pants and a pinkish-orange buttoned-up shirt sitting in a chair at the foot of the bed. "Who are you" Terry asked the man "Special Agent Hayden Alexander" Hayden replied as he showed Terry his badge "special agent" Terry asked confused "I'm a profiler for the JBI" Hayden told him "what do you want with me" Terry asked "first I would like you to tell me what happened yesterday" Hayden asked him "I can't remember" Terry replied "I believe you can, the doctors didn't find any concussions on you so I believe you do remember" Hayden told him "how bout an easier question, have you ever met a Dee-dee Simmons" Hayden asked him "the name doesn't sound familiar" Terry replied "how about the face" Hayden said as he put a picture of Dee-dee Simmons on Terry's lap for him to see, Terry looked at the picture "pretty eh well she ain't so pretty anymore" Hayden said to him. "Since you don't know her how bout Ann Miller" Hayden pressed him "no never heard of her either" Terry replied "here she is" Hayden said to him and put a picture of Ann Miller on his lap "what is this" Terry asked with a little agitation in his voice "are you sure you haven't met Ann, you sound a little doubtful" Hayden inquired. "I got nothing to say to you" Terry told Hayden "well then let me tell you something, we have your DNA and fingerprints tied to four murders so in a few minutes some men are coming in here to transfer you to the Mertle M Institution for the Criminal Insane, yes The Double M Terry that's where you'll be living until you get better then you'll be transferred to Greystone Maximum Prison for the rest of your life, but don't worry T you'll see me again real soon" Hayden informed him "leave me alone" Terry told Hayden in his stubbornness as he closed his eyes wanting to get back to sleep. Hayden collected the two pictures and then called for his JBI men out in the hallway to come in and arrest Terry and take him away, Hayden left the room as his men did so.

Two weeks later Terry was in a padded 9 feet by 10 feet room reading a Tennessee Williams novel, he was sitting on the bed in his blue cotton jump-suit and black slippers, that was the standard clothes for the patients at the Mertle M Institute. Terry was almost fully healed from his injuries, he was only experiencing joint-pain in his leg in which he had an a prescription for. Two stout and rangee-looking men dressed in all white came into Terry's room and put him in shackles, they brought him to a room down the hall, when they got to the room they sat him in one of two chairs that were around a round table, one of the men pad-locked Terry's shackles to a steel-chain that was bolted to the floor "wait there" he told Terry. Terry must of been in the room for a half an hour before Hayden walked in holding a file in a brown-paper folder, he sat down in the only empty chair in the room. Hayden placed the file on the table "I hope they treated you well here" Hayden said to Terry "what do you want from me" Terry asked Hayden "aw still in denial I see" Hayden said and continued "well just to inform you do to you getting better, in five days you'll be transferred to Greystone Maximum Prison, your stay at the Hilton-For-Cons has been shortened" Hayden said. "Do you feel what you do is right" Terry asked Hayden "I'm not too sure what you mean, can you clarify please" Hayden replied "this is harassment, I know it's harassment and so do you, I can have your badge for this" Terry told Hayden "Terry, for weeks I've been researching and studying who you are, so you might say I even know you, this thing that you're doing right now ain't your A-game, give me your A-game" Hayden informed him, Terry gave Hayden a cunning-smile "whatever you think you know about me you're way off" he told Hayden "I know you've never been married, you have no kids because raising kids and having a wife requires having and showing feelings and you are void of any feelings, most of the time you disguise that coldness with charm and humor like you tried with Dee-dee Simmons" Hayden told him "Agent Alexander whatever you read in that file means nothing to me" Terry told Hayden and looked away from him in disgust. Hayden shifted his chair closer to the round table that was between them "help me learn a little more" Hayden said to him "there's nothing to learn because I didn't do the things you said I did, I'm a taxidermist, all the stuff that you found is to do with taxidermy" Terry told him struggling to look into Hayden's eyes. Hayden gave out a short exhale of breath "Terry this is getting tiresome, lets talk about some of the stuff we found at your house in Umni" Hayden told him and continued "what's with all the old newsprint in your living room" Hayden asked him "I don't know what you're talking about" Terry replied "I believe I know why, there is a deep family secret that you don't quite know about but heard through the grapevine and ever since you've had these urges you've been collecting old newsprint to see where it came from, am I right" Hayden said to Terry. Terry started to get agitated "I wanna go back to my room, CAN I GO BACK TO MY ROOM" Terry called out to whomever was out in the hall "no one's out there, they all went to lunch" Hayden informed him "what the FUCK! DO YOU WANT FROM ME!" Terry screamed at Hayden "it's just eating you up inside to say, don't do this to yourself just get it out, you'll feel better" Hayden advised him. "as a kid you ever played the game 'Penny For Your Wishes'" Terry asked Hayden "yeah as a seven year old who hasn't" Hayden replied "well those are the rules from now on, starting with a Silver-piece" Terry told him, Hayden knew that there were a few vending-machines around and that

Terry would most likely use the money that he wins off him to get a snack from one of the machines "okay I'm game" Hayden said and put a Silver-piece on the table. Hayden looked at the file on the table "tell me about Dee-dee Simmons" he asked Terry "oh she was easy, the first time I met her was at a place in Amaryllis Jaiz called Slaps Bed & Breakfast, I use to drink at the bar their, one night she came over to the bar and we struck up a conversation, one thing led to another and we headed back to her place, on the way to her place she was getting out of hand so I kicked her out of my car near a variety-store" Terry told Hayden. Hayden kept the Silver-piece on the table and away from the reach of Terry "okay now tell me about Dana Hollinger" he ask Terry as he picked up the Silver-piece and put down a Janoesian Rupee (which is the same as one dollar) "yeah her, well if you want me to tell you about her it's going to cost you two Rupees" Terry told him "all I have is one" Hayden said "well I want two" Terry told him "fact of the matter is you aren't being totally honest, Dee-Dee didn't come onto you and you weren't going to her place, Dee-dee didn't know you, you stalked her and followed her from the BTM Theater the night you killed her" Hayden told Terry. Terry's facial expression went cold and he stared blankly at Hayden "so you're here to fix everything are you agent" Terry smartly asked him with a cynical tone in his voice, Hayden put the Rupee back in his pants pocket, he grabbed his file and stood up "well Terry my times up, it was nice speaking with you, in five day I'll be back to see your transfer through, I hope the next time we meet you have something better to tell me" Hayden told him and headed for the door "agent, this won't stop the horrors that happen on Janoesha Harbour each day" Terry said to Hayden as he opened the door "that's why the JBI is here" Hayden told him and left the room closing the door behind him.

Kimberly Anrhime is sitting in the board-room at the JBI building on 1 Tankanak Circle with Prussian Aubern a journalist for Channel 12 The Shore that broadcasts right here in Brookshore. Prussian was there asking Kimberly for the scoop on the Brookshore Ripper case, that is what the media was calling the murders done by Terry Willis, she also knew Kimberly from back in university so she figured as old friends she might have an opportunity to get a first-hand scoop on the case. "What do say Kim, it's just something to hold people over until the news breaks, we're getting calls from people at the news station that want to know what's going on with the Ripper case" she said to Kimberly "I'm sorry what was giving out to all the news stations is what you get for now, and we were never friends, just because we played on the same volleyball team didn't make us friends" Kimberly told her. "Can you at lease tell me where he is" Prussian asked Kimberly "sorry I can't tell you that, what I can tell you is the killer's name and his date of birth" Kimberly replied "okay that's something" Prussian said "his name is Terry Norman Willis born May 12th, 1969" Kimberly told her. After Prussian wrote down Terry's name on a pad of paper she asked Kimberly a question "do you know when his court date is and what court he's going to be tried in" "as you know this is a high profiled case, bodies were found in three different cities so it will take awhile for the courts to sort out the paper work, this is a federal case but all the bodies were in Passco Region so he will be tried at the Regional Court here in Brookshore" Kimberly replied. "Will the prosecution be asking for the death penalty" Prussian inquired "sorry I don't have that information" Kimberly told her "I heard that one of the dead women worked at one of the prosecutors firm, is this true" Prussian asked her "once again I don't have that information" Kimberly replied. Kimberly got up from sitting around the board-room table "that's it for the questions you had your five minutes" Kimberly told Prussian as she went to the board-room door opened it and stood beside the open door waiting for Prussian to leave. Prussian put away her pen and pad in a pocket of her army-green jacket and got up out of the chair she was sitting in, she headed for the open doorway of the board-room, as she left through the open doorway she turned and looked at Kimberly "thank you for your time" she said to her and left out the door heading down the hall to the elevator.

Five days had went by and Terry was looking better, he was almost a hundred percent. The institute's administrator had giving some patients chores to do, Terry was in the laundry-room folding clothes and table-cloths when two guards at the institution came into the room and put him in shackles "there's some people waiting to see you Terry" one of the guards told him. They escorted him to the front-lobby of the Mertle M Institute "what's this about, it's not my birthday so I know it's not a stripper" Terry asked jokingly with a smile on his face as he was being escorted to the front lobby "very funny" a guard replied. When Terry got to the front-lobby Hayden and James were there waiting for him "oh you again, when will you ever leave me alone" Terry sarcastically asked Hayden "it's good you have a sense of humor Terry, you're going to need it where you're going" Hayden told him as he signed his release-papers "who's your friend" Terry asked Hayden as he looked at James "Terry meet Special Agent James Morris of the JBI, he'll be accompanying me on your transfer" Hayden informed Terry as they took him from the guards. Hayden and James brought Terry out front to an armored Passco Regional Police van, there were to police officers sitting up front, one behind the wheel and the other in the passenger-seat, there was a double-barrel pump-action shotgun clipped on the door next to the officer in the passenger-seat. Hayden opened the van's back doors "okay Terry this is your ride, get on up in there" Hayden told Terry, Terry stepped up into the van with James following cautiously behind him, James pad-locked Terry's shackles to a steel-chain that was bolted to the floor of the van. Hayden got into the back of the van and closed the doors, he knocked on the side of the van indicating that they were ready to go, the van drove off. Hayden sat next to Terry and James sat across from him "it's going to be a good hour and a half until we get there" James informed Hayden after looking at his watch "yeah around that, they know we're on our way, a ferry will be waiting for us there" Hayden assured him. "Does anyone have a cigarette I can get off them I really like to smoke during road trips" Terry asked the two men "Sorry no smoking in the van" James told him as he pointed to the no smoking sign posted on the van's wall behind Terry "couldn't you just bend the rules this one time" Terry begged Hayden and James "if we did that we would be in the same position as you" Hayden told Terry. Terry smiled and let out a sly sounding chuckle "you like playing games do you Terry" James asked him already knowing the truth "aw it's going to be a long trip why not lighten the atmosphere a little" Terry said to James "so you don't care that you're going to be locked up for the rest of your life or receive the death penalty" James asked Terry "I don't even know what you guys are talking about, I'll have my day in court" Terry replied to James "hmm" James said as he studied Terry's facial expression and body-language. "At lease you're being honest, showing your real colors" Hayden said to Terry "did your dad teach you taxidermy" James asked Terry "yes he was a wonderful man, it's not until I went to pottery school I found a feel for it, to immolate the contours of the skull" Terry replied "how did you progress in that" James inquired "with bigger animals and going into business for myself" Terry replied "yeah but there's a point that you get tired of the same old thing, we're only human" James said to Terry "I was making okay money going into business for myself" Terry told James "I guess working at the hospital helped you with the animal-anatomy to" James said with a sarcastic tone in his voice "why do I even bother with you narrow-minded people" Terry said to James. "I'm sorry, so you never been married, no girlfriend, no kids" James asked Terry "that's right" Terry replied "the only dedication is your work" James said "that's right" Terry replied "can I ask why you didn't have a girlfriend" James inquired "just too focused on my studies and work" Terry replied "yeah but everyone has needs especially as a young adult" James inquired "well agent I'm guessing you weren't in the taxidermy business or living with my dad back in the 1980's and 90's" Terry asked James "no can't say I was" James replied "then I guess I have nothing else to say" Terry told James "what does having a girlfriend have to do with your father" James asked Terry but got no response. It had been forty-five minutes that the van had been on the road, they were now on Route 23 going into Tamerra, they stopped at an Oil/Mar gas station just outside Tamerra's city-limits for gas, while the driver filled up the gas-tank the passenger stood at the back-door of the van holding a shotgun and standing guard, they both were wearing bullet-proof vests. Hayden took the walkie talkie he had clipped onto his belt and radioed in to the driver "is everything okay up there" Hayden asked the driver "yes everything is okay I just stopped for gas" the driver answered "okay sounds good" Hayden said and hung up. The van started up again and continued its journey on Route 23, the driver had informed Hayden where they were "it won't be long now, another half an hour or so" Hayden told James "what's the matter agent you got a ball and chain at home" Terry interjected with a little cynicism in his voice "why is that feelings I detect in your voice Terry" Hayden asked Terry with a farce of concern in his voice. Terry gave Hayden a blank smile, "you know agent I might have to piss soon"

Terry said to Hayden "then you piss in that plastic-bottle at your feet" Hayden told him, there was a plastic soda bottle on its side next to Terry's left foot, Terry looked down at it "how respectful" he said to Hayden "thank you but that's more than you deserve" Hayden told him "that's not very nice agent and for all the time we've spent together these past five days I was thinking we were beginning to be friends" Terry said to Hayden with some farce in his voice "you have no friends Terry" Hayden told him. Forty minutes had gone by and they were at the ferry-dock to get to Greystone Prison, the van stopped at the dock, usually a prison-bus would come carrying twenty-five future inmates but this time was different, this was a special transfer of a wanted serial-killer. The two officers got out of the van and went around back and opened up the doors, Hayden hopped out of the back of the van followed by Terry and then James, one of the officers closed back the doors. "Okay Terry, James and these two officers are going to be taking you the rest of the way, now if you want to know when your trial begins I don't have that information, but if I were to guess I would say not for a few months but then again you can always talk with your lawyer" Hayden informed Terry "agent do you believe in karma, that the earth's a ball and everything rotates" Terry asked Hayden "you have all the time you need to tell your theories to your cell-mate" Hayden told Terry and then motioned with his hand for the officers to take him, Terry looked back at Hayden as the officers escorted him to the police-ferry waiting for them "give me a call when you're on your way back and let me know how it went" Hayden told James "sure thing" James replied and left to catch up with the officers.

Eleven months had gone by and Terry's court case had been over for the past two months, Terry was sentenced to death by the gas-chamber, he was to be executed in three weeks, a couple of days ago he asked to speak with Special Agent Hayden Alexander. Terry has his own eight by nine feet cell on death-row, two extremely large and muscular prison guards came to Terry's cell to escort him to the prison's visitor's booths. Visitor's Booths are a line of six three by five feet booths made for prisoners to come and speak with their family and friend or with a lawyer, there is a four inch thick wall of plexy-glass dividing the prisoner from the visitor but only from the shoulders up, from the shoulders down is a regular concrete-wall. The guards came in Terry's cell "how you doing today fellas" Terry asked the guards while he was sitting on his bed and closed the book he was reading "you have a visitor Terry" one of the guards told him. The guards put shackles on Terry "time to go" one of them told Terry, they brought Terry to the visitor's booths and sat him down in a chair in booth number three, one guard pad-locked his shackles to a steel-chain that was bolted to the floor. Terry saw that it was Hayden sitting across from him on the other side of the plexy-glass "I received your request to see me" Hayden told Terry "funny I don't remember seeing you at my court case agent" Terry said to Hayden "there was no need for me to be there" Hayden replied "agent why do you think someone would do the things that I did, because I really don't know" Terry asked Hayden, the strange thing was Hayden could see in Terry's eyes that it was a genuine question that Terry was asking because he truly didn't know why he did the things he did "I believe it started as an experiment and during the course of the experiment you discovered that you have these urges, so your acts were to fulfill your urges" Hayden explained to Terry "hmm, profiler eh" Terry said "that's correct" Hayden replied "do you really think it's that" Terry asked Hayden "yes I do, but like a drug you wanted more so you took more and you couldn't stop so you started stalking your prey sometimes for a day or two before you striked" Hayden told him. Terry gave Hayden a cold-stare with a smile on his face "I guess that's why you make the big bucks" Terry said to Hayden "why did you request to see me, I know you don't need me to profile you, you already know the monster you are" Hayden asked Terry "do you think God can forgive someone like me" Terry asked Hayden "I'm not in any position to elaborate on that" Hayden replied "I know but I would like to hear what you think" Terry told him "I believe God forgives those who ask for forgiveness and except that they've done wrong" Hayden replied. Terry looked down at his feet like he had something weighing on his mind, he raised up his head after a few seconds "I started reading the Holy Bible, trying to make things right spiritually ya know" he told Hayden "that's good Terry, how do you feel innerly" Hayden asked Terry, Terry laughed and waved his index-finger at Hayden "you're good agent, nothing gets by you eh" Terry said to Hayden "Terry you're a sociopath, the only fulfillment a sociopath has is to himself" Hayden told Terry "well I called you here agent to tell you that I except what I've done but can I ask you something agent, in court they charged me for killing four people, are you sure it's only four people I killed" Terry asked Hayden with a blank expression on his face "no Terry I'm not sure, but I know you're fifty-three years old and a person like you doesn't begin killing in his early fifties, we still suspect that there's more bodies out there, these four we had a lot of evidence on and DNA, plus you have a signature and we know it now so if any human remains pop up with that signature we know who to match it to" Hayden replied. Hayden thought about a case that came to his desk about five months ago, some human remains were found off a logging road in a cluster of fern and palm-bushes near Pebble River just west of southwest Pearles, the medical examiner told him that they look to be of a young lady, they also found tattered clothing nearby. "I can help you agent" Terry said to Hayden "perhaps you can but I cannot reverse the decision on your execution, so if that's what you're looking for I'm sorry" Hayden told him "but you can hold it off until a later date, can't you" Terry asked Hayden "why would I want to do that" Hayden asked him "you and I both know that I didn't just kill four women, what if I offer to show you where some are buried" Terry said to Hayden "normally serial killers will go back to where they committed the murder to re-live it, is that what this is about" Hayden asked Terry "no not at all, I just need some time to make it right with God and do something good for a change" Terry replied. Hayden knew that Terry was very clever and had an eye for detail 'what if this was a clever way of plotting an escape' he thought to himself "well Terry as tempting as that sounds we have your fingerprints and DNA plus your in prison for life or at lease until you are executed so you see that's the max someone can get on Janoesha Harbour, and for the families of missing love ones when we find their remains and connect it back to you, their families will be glad to know you have been executed" Hayden told him and got up from out of the chair he was sitting in "well my time is up and I gotta get back to my office" Hayden told Terry as he turned around and headed for the door "where are you going" Terry asked Hayden "back to work" Hayden replied without turning around "GET BACK HERE AGENT, THIS IS NOT OVER" Terry screamed at Hayden as Hayden opened the door "it is for me, have a nice afterlife" Hayden said and left the room.

THE END

Printed in the United States
by Baker & Taylor Publisher Services